THE REDHEAD MOANED, DIGGING HER MANICURED NAILS INTO CAPTAIN GRINGO'S BARE BACK...

Then, just as they were coming back down from heaven, all hell broke loose outside!

Meabh stiffened in terror under him as the night was rent by the mad chatter of a machine gun, firing full automatic, and close! Captain Gringo rolled off her, grabbed his .38, and moved to open the tent flap just enough to see what was going on.

What was going on was someone pumping hot Maxim lead, lots of hot Maxim lead, at a target Gringo couldn't see. But he could see the muzzle flash, firing inside the camp. So he trained his .38 on it and called out, "Knock that off! I won't say it twice!"

The muzzle of the machine gun swung his way, still firing, as it sought out the sound of his voice with rapid-fire death ..

Novels by
Ramsay Thorne

Published by
WARNER BOOKS

Renegade #27

SAVAGE SAFARI

Ramsay Thorne

WARNER BOOKS

A Warner Communications Company

WARNER BOOKS EDITION

Copyright © 1984 by Lou Cameron
All rights reserved.

Warner Books, Inc.
666 Fifth Avenue
New York, N.Y. 10103

 A Warner Communications Company

Printed in the United States of America

First Printing: November, 1984

10 9 8 7 6 5 4 3 2 1

Captain Gringo was only human. So when he met a big black fuzzy monster in a dark alley, he naturally knocked it flat with a left hook, kicked it flatter with a mosquito boot, and seriously considered shooting it. But by the time he had his gun out, he'd spotted what looked like a torchlight parade coming down the alley at him, too, and decided this was hardly the time for a man with a price on his head and no valid passport in his pocket to be hanging around. So he naturally started running like hell.

Behind him, he heard a voice in the crowd shout, "Mira! *Take* him, muchachos!" And while it wasn't clear from the ominous roar of the crowd whether they meant him or whatever he'd just tangled with, he didn't want to find out until everyone had cooled down some. So he crabbed sideways into a slot between two buildings, then cursed as he saw he was boxed in a coffin-wide cul-de-sac!

The stucco wall blocking his escape was a bit lower than the house walls on either side. But he still had a hell of a time getting over it. He lost his planter's hat as he grabbed the gritty top of the wall on the third try and hauled himself over to drop blindly into the patio or whatever on the far side. He could tell he'd timed it close as, looking up, he saw the brimstone glow of torchlight flickering on the stucco above. He sat still as a mouse in the long grass he'd landed in, drawing his .38 once more as he tried to make out what they were muttering about on the far side. But too many people were muttering too many things at once, and all that really mattered was that, so far, nobody seemed to be coming over

1

the wall after him and, miracle of miracles, the voices were even fading away as the mob moved on, back, or some damned where.

He waited anyway, until he'd said "Mississippi" a hundred times just to make sure. Then he got to his feet, hoping to figure out where he was. There had to be a better way out of here than back over that wall. Planter's hats were a hell of a lot cheaper than his head.

It was black as the inside of a cat, now that the torchbearers had moved away. There wasn't one illuminated window facing the dark, grassy void he'd lucked into. He sensed it was a little too large to be the patio he'd first taken it for. He didn't mind. Explaining what one was doing in someone's patio at midnight could be a pain in the ass. He put his free hand against rough stucco and started following the wall clockwise. There had to be a door or gateway somewhere.

He made it to a corner, and so now he had to be heading for the far side of the block he'd been dumb enough to cut through late at night in a strange town. His hotel couldn't be more than five blocks away. If only he could find a way out of this mysterious black pit. He barked his shin on something solid in front of him. He put his .38 back into its shoulder holster and took out a box of waterproof matches. He took a deep breath and struck a light. Then he muttered, "Jesus, this sure is a night for neat shortcuts!"

He was standing in a graveyard, at midnight, after just having had a run-in with a spook. He laughed anyway as he shook out the match and kept going. Looking on the bright side, real people hardly ever visited graveyards in the middle of a dark, moonless night, and, what the hell, he'd just flattened the biggest spook he'd ever seen around here!

He thought about that as he worked his way along the wall and over more than one grave. The brief encounter in that alley hadn't lasted long enough for him to have made a lasting impression of the whatever he'd decked. He tried to recall more detail. There wasn't much to recall. One minute he'd been strolling through a dark alley, minding his own business; and, the next thing he'd known, a moaning apparition had loomed out of the gloom at him.

Its big black fuzzy arms had been spread as if to grab him. So the sucker punch had been easy. But what in the hell had he punched? Maybe an ape that had busted loose from some zoo? That would explain all those guys chasing it. A man-size ape running loose could make people nervous.

But did they have a zoo in Puerto Nogales? From what he'd seen of the little seaport so far, they didn't even have streetlights or a for God's sake tobacco shop within five blocks of what Gaston had said was the best hotel in town!

He found his way to the fancy, albeit rusty, wrought-iron gate. It was locked. He peered through, saw the calle on the far side was almost as dark as where he was, and simply climbed over it. He looked both ways. Nobody seemed to be looking for him. A steam whistle to his right gave him his bearings. He shrugged and headed back to the waterfront. So much for going out to buy smokes late at night in Puerto Nogales. If Gaston was still out when he got back to the hotel, Captain Gringo wasn't going to mention this adventure. The small, gray semi-invisible Frenchman had warned him not to wander around on his own here. Puerto Nogales was said to be a tough little town. Captain Gringo wasn't sure how tough it was, but it sure seemed well named, when one considered nogales were a kind of *nut*!

He saw light ahead. The calle he was following led him to the waterfront where weary-looking peones were still loading bananas on that same shelter-deck steamer by the same lantern light. He knew where he was now. He turned the corner and passed a squalid little cantina that, alas, sold neither tobacco nor, indeed, drinks fit for human consumption.

He strode on to the waterfront hotel Gaston had chosen, he said, for its view of the Caribbean and for cross-ventilation. The tall American went up the outside stairs, tried the door, then grinned and took out his key as he saw he'd beaten his sidekick home.

Inside, the room they'd taken did seem a little cooler now. He struck another match to light the candle provided by the management. They'd not only never heard of Thomas Edison in Puerto Nogales, they'd apparently never heard of coal-oil lamps, either. But what could one expect of a town named after walnuts—when even a gringo like Captain Gringo knew walnuts didn't grow along the mangrove-haunted Mosquito Coast of Honduras.

They hadn't been able to book two rooms. They'd been lucky to get one fair-size room with brass beds against opposite walls. But at least the best hotel in Puerto Nogales had indoor plumbing. Sort of. So he stepped into the tiny bathroom, lit another candle over the sink, and took a leak in the commode. It flushed on the second try.

As he washed his hands at the sink, he noticed he'd stained his knuckles with something black. He tried the cheap soap and saw that whatever it was didn't want to come off. It looked like black paint or maybe roofing tar. That worked. He'd been climbing over lots of stuff that needed protection from the damp, humid trade winds they had around here.

By using more soap and rubbing harder, he got most of it off. Anything that wouldn't come off with soap and water wasn't going to come off on the sheets, and the sheets weren't his anyway, so what the hell.

He'd just finished drying his hands and buttoning up his fly when Gaston came in from wherever the hell he'd been. Gaston was not alone. The little old Legion deserter had a mestiza girl clinging coyly to either arm. Neither one was ever going to make the cover of the *Police Gazette*. But, on the other hand, no lady looks all that bad in a low-cut peasant blouse by candlelight after a guy's been at sea almost a week and doesn't know another soul in town.

Gaston said, "Look what followed me home, Dick. This adorable child who says she admires older men is Rosalita. I think you would get along better with Floralinda here, non?"

Floralinda giggled, disengaged from the older man, and came over to snuggle against Captain Gringo. She was the younger and prettier of the pair, if one didn't mind an occasional gold tooth. Captain Gringo put a casual arm around her but asked Gaston in English, "What about the evolution-ray?"

Gaston shrugged and said, "It seems to be off. When I went to contact the people we were to join, there were some très fatigué Honduran army types loitering about the premises. So I did not think it wise to go in, hein?''

''Jesus, they've been picked up, and we're just standing here like big-ass birds?''

''Mais non, we are behaving as the innocent-looking species of beachcombers one sincerely hopes we may be taken for until that banana boat down the quay is ready to leave, of course. If there was another, quicker way out of here, I assure you I would have found it. Meanwhile, on my way here I thought it wise to stop at a friendly home for wayward girls and order these two, to go.''

It wouldn't have been polite to grimace in distaste at a lady who was rubbing her considerable charms against him at the moment. It wasn't even polite to go on talking in English. But he had to as he growled, ''God damn it, Gaston. We don't have the money to spare, even if I paid for my pussy!''

Gaston chuckled dryly and replied, ''There are times to be romantique and times to be practique. I've already paid their madame. So try to pretend it's true love. We have to have *some* excuse for having booked this room instead of staying aboard our ship until it's loaded, hein?''

Suiting actions to his words, Gaston snuffed out the candle and led his older puta to his own bed, saying to her in Spanish, ''Let me help you, Querida. Sacre, is all of that *you*, under that adorable skirt?''

Captain Gringo found himself standing in the dark with Floralinda and, from the way she was fumbling at his pants, she seemed in need of guidance too. So he laughed and said, ''I'll get you for this, Gaston!'' as he led her to his own bed. Or tried to. By the time they got there, Floralinda was sort of leading him, by the dong. As she sat down on the bed, still holding it, she sighed and asked, ''What is the matter? Don't you like me?''

He laughed again and said, ''I'm still thinking about it. Are you always this direct, Floralinda?''

He knew it was a silly question. But he had to say something with a lady holding him by a limp leash. Floralinda pulled him closer to reply by kissing its confused head, and then—as she took it into her warm, wet mouth and proceeded to slide her soft pursed lips up and down the full length of his shaft—that part of him, at least, was no longer confused.

But the rest of him still felt a little silly as he stood there undressing himself in the dark as she blew French tunes on his rapidly rising love flute. He got rid of everything but his gun rig and boots. Then he shoved her over backward, growled, "Hey, how come you're still dressed?" and proceeded to lay her right, with her skirts up around her waist and her plump legs around his waist.

She liked it, or said she did. It was hard to tell with businesswomen. But she sure moved her hips as good as she could move her head, and pursed her lips down there pretty good, too. So he exploded in her almost at once, and since it really had been a long, boring sea voyage, with another one facing them in the morning if they lived that long, he didn't stop.

Floralinda giggled and told her invisible chum across the room, in a surprisingly conversational tone, "This one is muy toro indeed! How are you making out, Rosalita?"

Gaston replied, "She can't answer right now. But she seems to like older men as much as she said. Et now, if you children will forgive me, I must get back to my meal."

Floralinda giggled and told Captain Gringo they were going sixty-nine. He asked himself what else was new. He didn't answer. As a lay, she wasn't bad. But he was damned if he intended to even kiss her *mouth*, all things considered. So he just kept humping, and if she didn't like it, tuff.

She said, "Wait, let me get out of these clothes so we can do it right. You have been at sea awhile, have you not?"

He said he sure had, wondering what else Gaston had told them, as he rolled off to let her shuck her blouse and skirt. He was surprised at himself for wanting more. He knew he should be a little disgusted. But as she pulled him back aboard her voluptuous and now stark-naked body, he decided to forgive Gaston. There were worse ways than this to fool the local law, and if they didn't fool it good, old Floralinda figured to be the last dame he was ever going to have. So he decided to have all she had to offer; and she offered a lot, for a pro.

She didn't try to kiss him, bless her professional delicacy, as she moaned that she too was climaxing and, whether it was true or not, gave a most convincing performance with her internal muscles. He just enjoyed it, not questioning the few sordid luxuries of the so-far disgusting little port of call. So he was mildly surprised when she sighed and told her chum across the room, "I can't believe it, Rosalita. But I just came!"

Her unseen companion answered in a husky, bemused voice, "Me too. A considerate customer is such a nice change. And to think we have the whole night with these two alone!"

"Let's make it a party," said Floralinda, grinding her groin teasingly against Captain Gringo as he lay limp in her love saddle, sated for the moment. He muttered, "Jesus, I don't even have any cigars to smoke between times. Let a guy get his breath back, at least."

She insisted, "Get off. We are going to play musical cunts. Do you know that game, Querido?"

"I think I know how it's played. Are you following all this, Gaston?"

"Mais oui, with considerable interest. But first some rules of the ground, non? I am as good a sport as any Frenchman. But once another man has dipped his spoon in the bouillabaisse, I tend to lose my appetite for seafood!"

Floralinda laughed and said, "Do not speak tonto. Oral sex is for to inspire bashful married men. It is not often we get a pair of hard-up sailors who like for to fuck!"

Rosalita must have agreed with her. For the next thing Captain Gringo knew, she'd dragged poor Gaston over to join them. The older, plumper whore climbed on Captain Gringo's bed, near the foot, and remained on her hands and knees there as she said, simply, "Bueno. Somebody put it *in* me, damn it!"

Gaston said, "I wish you would, Dick. Even with fresh inspiration, I am not sure what sort of monster I have created here!"

Captain Gringo laughed, rolled to his feet, and moved behind the bigger rump of Rosalita as Floralinda giggled and assumed the same position side by side with the older whore. Captain Gringo muttered, "This is getting silly," as he entered Rosalita dog-style to see Gaston doing the same to Floralinda right next to him. Then, as he got all the way into what old Rosalita had to offer, he grabbed her ample hips and added, "But it ain't bad!" as he and Gaston proceeded to hump them in unison while the two whores chatted casually. Apparently they genuinely liked good sex. But after agreeing the change in partners was interesting, they got down to discussing something about the way their laundry was being mistreated by some Chinaman they both seemed annoyed at.

Gaston chuckled and said, "Eh bien, this makes me homesick. It reminds me of the time I worked as a bouncer in a place my Great Aunt Yvette ran, near the Moulin Rouge."

"Okay, I can post in the saddle and talk at the same time, too. So tell me about that banana boat. Have you fixed it with the purser yet?"

"Mais non. When I saw the revolutionary headquarters guarded by the wrong side, I of course ducked into the nearest whorehouse. And the rest you know. They must like us, the adorable children. They never chat like this when entertaining the usual contemptible romantiques."

Captain Gringo wasn't trying to follow the conversation in Spanish as the two whores chatted with their heads down on the mattress and their rumps in the air. The two soldiers of fortune went on speaking in English, of course, as Captain Gringo said, "Don't even mention evolution-ray, even in English, damn it. How long do we have to keep this nonsense up?"

"I don't know. I can fuck for hours, pacing myself like this. It won't be safe to approach the steamboat purser before dawn. I did ask one of the stevedores when they would be shoving off. He said they hoped to have the holds filled by then. Speaking of filling holds, would you excuse me a moment? I seem to be climaxing in this adorable little playmate of yours!"

Captain Gringo laughed as the small but virile Frenchman started pounding what was hardly *his* playmate at the moment to glory; and, from the way Floralinda was moving, she too seemed to have forgotten her old friends. The one he had his own bemused semi-erection in hissed, "Faster! Faster! They're getting ahead of us, Sailor!"

He did his best to oblige, feeling a little better now. For not only did their casual pickups rut like the simple healthy animals they were, neither had they bothered to remember any *names*!

Captain Gringo was not only big and strong, but well hung and, in truth, not as interested in what he was doing to Rosalita as he might have been had not he had other things to worry about. So she came well ahead of him and announced it loudly—as Floralinda, probably showing off at least a bit, replied, "Me too! Madre de Dios! They both fuck so good!"

Outside, on the steps, one uniformed Honduran who'd crept up on them turned to the one who'd crept after him and chuckled, "Have you heard enough, Pedro?"

The other suppressed a louder laugh and replied, "Si, it was as the madame said. Just a couple of sailors with a couple of her whores. Come on, we still have to find those soldiers of fortune."

They started to move away. Then the first one said, "Wait. I hear the two men talking. They are speaking in *English*. Do you think the Lieutenant might find that interesting?"

"For why? We already knew they were off that banana boat from New Orleans. What would you expect Yanqui seamen to speak, Chinese? Let's go. Listening to all that rutting is giving me a hard-on, and you are just not my type."

So they moved silently down the steps as, upstairs, the two whores insisted on changing partners again and the two soldiers of fortune made some rather crude comments, again in English, as they went along with the game. The two soldiers were joined by a third as they stepped out on the quay. He said, "New orders from the Lieutenant. We are to keep our eyes peeled for a big blond Yanqui wearing a planter's hat. He was spotted earlier tonight, here in Puerto Nogales, and he answers to the description of the notorious Captain Gringo, Ricardo Walker!"

One of the two who'd checked out the hotel looked

thoughtfully back the way they'd just come and mused aloud, "Hmm, that one sailor is most big and blond, no?"

But his partner said, "Half of them are big and blond. The one up there does not wear any kind of hat. They told us that at the cantina just now, remember?"

The soldier who'd just joined them said, "I have an idea. For why don't we just ask them at the banana boat whether they have two crewmen getting laid at the hotel, eh?"

They all thought that was a swell idea and headed down the quay as, blissfully unaware of the danger they were in at the moment, Captain Gringo and Gaston went on making love, or showing off, with Rosalita and Floralinda.

The girls seemed to have some kind of follow-the-leader challenge in mind by this time. So Captain Gringo was once more laying Floralinda—or would have been if they hadn't been doing it standing up against the wall for some weird reason. Gaston, after pointing out it wasn't fair, since his legs were shorter, had Rosalita draped over the brass footrails of the nearby bed in an ingenious position; and as everyone moved sensuously but by now with calm determination, the two girls were dishing another whore they didn't like. They agreed she thought she was hot stuff but that in God's truth she was a frigid bitch, etc.

Captain Gringo muttered, "You know what? My legs are getting tired and this is really weird. I'm ready to concede any time you are, Gaston."

Gaston said, "Oui. Let me finish, this way. I told you before we got here that the whole situation up this way was très weird. I can't wait to get out of here. Out of this port, I mean. Where I am at the *moment* is not bad and, ah, oui, this angle is très amusé, non?"

"How the hell should I know? I'm doing it to a different broad at a different angle. Speaking of weird—I forgot to tell you, but I ran into some other weird stuff earlier tonight. Do they have man-size apes in Central America, Gaston?"

"I don't think so. Tell me about it later. Oh, you really must try Rosalita in this position, Dick!"

Rosalita seemed to think that was a swell idea, too. So when Floralinda suggested changing partners again, the older, plumper Rosalita simply stayed as she was, perched atop the brass rail with a bare foot hooked against either bedpost, open for business indeed.

Captain Gringo sighed and said, "No shit, Gaston. I want to tell you about a funny thing that happened to me in an alley tonight."

But then he saw he was outvoted. So as Gaston led Floralinda around to assume a more sedate position on the mattress behind Rosalita, Captain Gringo muttered, "Jesus, the things you get me into, Gaston," and got in Rosalita again. Then he hissed in pleased surprise and grabbed the brass on either side of her ample hips as he found himself more inspired by this new position than he'd expected.

Meanwhile, down the quay, the skipper of the banana boat stood smoking on the bridge wing as the three soldiers approached the gangplank below.

The skipper neither spoke nor wanted to learn Spanish. So he yelled down, "What do you greasers want?"

Only one of the three soldiers spoke any English at all, and he, most fortunately, didn't speak it well enough to know what a "greaser" might or might not be. He called up, "We are military police, Señor! We wish for to know if you have allowed any of your crew ashore tonight."

The skipper spat and said, "Sure I have. What's it to you?"

"Perhaps nothing, Señor. It all depends. Could you tell us if you have a tall blond man, about thirty, and a smaller darker man, perhaps fifty or sixty, in your crew?"

"Sure. That sounds like Butch and Smitty. What have they done?"

The soldier laughed and called back, "Nothing a sailor in a strange port of call has never done before. We only wished for to make sure they were your men. Muchas gracias, Señor."

As the soldiers walked away, a mate came out from the pilot house to ask what was going on. The skipper said, "That big blond kid, Butch, went to get drunk with little Smitty tonight, right?"

The mate said, "Smitty went ashore awhile, Sir. But he's back on board now, if you need him."

"I don't need Smitty. Them greasers were just asking about him and old Butch. Is Butch still ashore?"

The mate shook his head and said, "Never went ashore here, Skipper. Saw him just a little while ago in the galley, drinking coffee for a change and not enjoying it much. Old Butch is low on shore money until we get paid off next week. So whatever the greasers say he done, he never done it."

The Skipper stared thoughtfully after the three Honduran soldiers down the quay. They were still in sight but out of easy hailing distance by this time. He took a drag on his smoke and said, "That's funny. How could they be asking anything about a couple of our guys if our guys ain't anywhere ashore?"

The mate followed his gaze and asked, "Want me to go after 'em and check it out, Skipper?"

The skipper started to nod, shrugged instead, and said, "Fuck 'em. It ain't *our* problem."

It was just as well neither Captain Gringo nor Gaston had any idea that the winning side was scouring Puerto Nogales and the surrounding swamps for any sign of them by the dawn's early light. For neither soldier of fortune was in any shape to run, even had there been any place to run to.

The two exhausted whores were paying for their own showing off, fast asleep, when Captain Gringo opened one eye, saw grim, gray daylight winking through the window shutters at him, and groaned, "Gaston, you lazy old bastard. Get up and see about sneaking us aboard that banana boat before it leaves."

Gaston told him to do something that was not only perverse but physically impossible, adding, "The species of boat will not be pulling out this early. Wake me at nine, you boisterous youth!"

"Wake up, damn it! How do you know what time they

figure to cast off? I thought you hadn't spoken to anyone aboard yet."

"Merde alors, have you never heard time and tide go together in a shallow-draft seaport, Dick?"

"Oh, right. They will be leaving with the tide and, let's see . . . yeah, nine-thirty sounds about right. But stay awake anyway. We've got things to chat about."

"Discuss them with your athletique species of bed partner. Thanks to the two of them, I ache in every one of my adorable old bones; and if you can think of another grotesque position to screw either of them in, please don't tell me about it!"

"Damn it, this is the first time I've been able to talk to you when you weren't playing slap and tickle, Gaston. I told you I tangled with an ape or something in an alley last night. I've been thinking about that a lot. You're right: there just isn't anything bigger than a howler monkey running loose down here. But the ape I met up with stood at least six feet. Worse yet, a mess of guys were chasing it. They might have wound up chasing me, too. So how do we check that out?"

Gaston propped himself up on one elbow, shoving Rosalita's plump thigh off his lap as he rubbed a weary hand over his sleep-gummed eyes. The whore murmured in her sleep and rolled her face to the wall as she farted loudly. Gaston said, "If I was not awake before, I am *now*! Sacre God damn! I need *air*!"

He rolled out of bed, naked, and threw open the blinds. Then he shut them again quickly and said softly, "Army patrol, big one, marching past along the quay."

Captain Gringo nudged his own bed partner to ask how she felt about breakfast. She moaned and turned on her belly to sleep more soundly. He swung his naked feet to the floor and said, "Bueno. We don't have to feed 'em, and I sure as hell don't want to fuck anyone for at least a month."

He reached under the bed to haul out his oilcloth satchel, fumbled under the duds he'd piled on the bed table for his gun rig, and rose to go into the bathroom as Gaston risked another cautious peek through the shutters and muttered,

"Merde alors, I didn't know they had that many men in the très fatigué garrison here!"

Captain Gringo tested the hot-water tap. He hadn't expected hot water at this hour. So he shrugged, wet a hotel towel good, and gave himself a quick, tepid whore bath as he studied his face in the cracked mirror and decided he could get away without shaving this morning in such crummy surroundings. He rinsed his mouth out with snake-bite remedy from his little traveling kit and was drying off when Gaston joined him to ask, "Are we going somewhere, my foolish youth? I just told you the quay is très lousy avec troops!"

The taller American replied, "I heard you. So what? For once we seem to be ahead of the game. We've got the front money they wired us back in San Jose. We can't contact rebels that have already lost their revolution, so we've lived up to our part of the contract the easy way for a change."

"Your logique is perfect, up to one small point, Dick. I agree it makes sense to take the money and run. Mais, the moment we step outside, we may have to run faster than a man my age is capable of! Before you make any silly remarks about heading for the border via the très amusé jungle, I told you before we got here that Puerto Nogales is surrounded by jungle of a particularly alarming nature, hein?"

"That's good. If there's no way out of here cross-country, the army has things under control and, more important, knows it has things under control. You'd better wash your crotch, at least, before we talk to the purser of that banana boat. You smell like an old whore."

Gaston took a fresh towel to wet as he told Captain Gringo he was crazy. But by the time they'd both cleaned off and got into shape to clear out, the quay outside seemed clear again. As Gaston put his own linen jacket on over his gun rig, he asked Captain Gringo how he'd known that miracle would come to pass. Captain Gringo said, "Easy. I've led troops through more than one Indian village in my time. Guys massed and marching aren't searching. They've already searched and reassembled to march somewhere else."

"They don't seem to have searched this hotel yet. I'm sure I would have noticed, even eating pussy."

"They checked. Down at the desk, at the very least. Obviously, and as we hoped, a couple of non-Latin names shacked up with a couple of local whores didn't read 'Honduran rebel' to them. Let's go. We've time for breakfast, and I'm hungry as a bitch wolf for some reason."

They left the two girls in the arms of Morpheus—who was more than welcome to them, now that they'd seen them by the cold, gray light of a soggy morning—and eased down the outside steps, carrying their scanty luggage. They both agreed it seemed impolite to bother the management about checking out when the room had been paid for until noon.

The cantina just down the quay was open twenty-four hours a day, bless it, and was not too crowded at this hour. So they took a dark corner table and asked the sleepy-looking waitress if they could get anything to eat to go with their cerveza. She said they could have beans with rice or rice with beans. Captain Gringo said beans with rice sounded fine, and Gaston, just to be different, ordered rice and beans.

Most of the other customers seemed to be native stevedores, just finished a night's work. Nobody worked the docks under the tropic sun in this part of the world unless it was important as hell, for double pay. A handful of seamen off the various vessels in the harbor were trying to sober up with black coffee at other tables here and there. Nobody seemed to be paying any attention to the two soldiers of fortune or anything else. So, as they waited for their order, Gaston murmured, "Eh bien, those troops we were worried about have not been bothering innocent bystanders. They must have made a clean sweep after all. I wonder how? The people who hired us could not be the ones who informed on them, hein?"

Captain Gringo growled, "Forget ancient history and you won't blab about it at the wrong time. It doesn't matter how the local military caught on so soon. They did. So all we have to worry about is a discreet exit, stage left or, hell, right, as long as we get our asses *out* of here!"

The waitress brought their beers and breakfasts. She must have compared Captain Gringo to the other guys in the place by now, for she looked wider awake and even managed a smile as she said, "Some night we had, no?"

He grinned up at her and replied gallantly, "I wish we had. But you weren't on duty last night when I really needed you, Señorita . . . ah?"

"I am called Inez." She dimpled, adding with a mocking laugh, "But I am not that kind of a girl. I was referring to all the excitement with those rebels."

Captain Gringo picked up his beer schooner to swallow silently. But Gaston asked her to tell them about it before Captain Gringo could kick him under the table.

So the waitress—damn Gaston—sat down across from them on a free stool and told Captain Gringo rather than Gaston, "They think it was an attempted coup against our provincial governor, Don Nogales. Naturally they were betrayed, and naturally the army arrested them all before they could do anything bad to our landlord and protector. I was off duty until just about an hour ago, so naturally I went for to watch the executions."

Captain Gringo saw she expected him to say something. So he nodded and said, "I was wondering why you looked so tired. More exciting than a bullfight, eh?"

She grimaced, and he liked her a little better when she replied, "In God's truth, had I known they were going to treat them so brutally, I would not have gone. I mean, I know rebels deserve to die, but to tar and feather a man, then make him dig his own grave in agony—"

"Hey, I'm eating breakfast, Inez!"

"I am sorry. You are right. I did not get much sleep last night, afterwards. I know our Don Nogales had to set a stern example. But I do not think I shall attend any more of his public executions in the future."

Gaston swallowed a mouthful of food and asked soberly, "Have they said anything about a repeat performance, Señorita Inez?"

She shrugged and said, "I hope not. I think they shot them all. One burst free just as they were about to shoot him. But he did not get away. They found him unconscious in an alley. He must have fainted from the pain. I left about then. I mean no disrespect to our governor, but I could not help feeling at least a little pity when they buried him with the others, alive. Many of us thought they should have shot him first, but who are we to argue with our betters, eh?''

An angry male voice called her name, and Inez rose, saying, ''I have to get back to work. I get off at noon, señor...?''

''I am called Ricardo.''

''Bueno. Perhaps we can talk some more then, unless you are off that banana boat bound for New Orleans.''

Captain Gringo kept his face blank as he asked, ''Do I look like a man who wants to go to New Orleans, Querida?''

She laughed, told him not to be fresh, and headed back to the kitchen. Gaston said, ''Not bad. She's prettier than the breakfast they serve here. But do you really think she's worth missing the next ship out, Dick?''

''A ship bound directly for the States? I'd give that a miss if she had two heads and no tits! How can we check on that, Gaston? A banana boat making stops along the Mosquito Coast is one thing. A banana boat putting out to beeline for New Orleans just won't do!''

Gaston shrugged and said, ''Going through U.S. Customs with a U.S. army death warrant on one's adorable head could be très fatigué. Mais, observe how smart I am.''

He turned on his stool to nudge a burly Negro seated at the next table and ask, ''Perdone Usted, Señor, were you not the jefe of the stevedores who loaded all those bananas last night, down the quay?''

The native blinked in pleased surprise and replied with a laugh, ''I wish I had been. My back would feel better this morning. I mean no disrespect, but if you caballeros are off that Yanqui tub, your skipper is a child molester and I don't think his mother's safe from him, either!''

Gaston laughed easily and said, ''We heard he was a bastard to work for. You may have saved us a fool's errand. But we heard he was heading from here directly back to New Orleans, and if that is so, we may have to risk our poor assholes.''

The friendly Negro nodded understandingly and said, ''On the beach, eh? Well, I don't have to tell you how hard it is for

Yanquis to get a berth home once they lose one. So maybe you can get along with the bastard better than we could. You'll have to if you're homesick. There's not another vessel leaving directly for Los Estados Unidos due out of here this week.''

"Eh bien, perhaps we'd better have a word with the monster. May we buy you a drink, Amigo?''

The stevedore nodded. Then, since he really was a nice guy, shook his head and said, "No thanks. You'd better wait until you see if that hard-nosed Yanqui skipper will hire you before you spend any more money than you have to. I'm not going to buy you a drink, either. Once word gets around about a revolution, business can get slow in any port of call, if you know what I mean.''

"Oui, when a tramp steamer can put in anywhere for the same cargo, why risk broken portholes? But we heard the dramatiques were over, here in Puerto Nogales.''

The stevedore shrugged and replied, "I sure hope so. I have a wife and four children to feed. But some soldados I was talking to just a little while ago told me they're still looking for at least two rebel leaders who got away.''

"Oh? What did they say these ogres looked like, in case we run into them?''

The Negro shrugged and said, "Just a couple of the usual soldados de fortuna. One big blanco. One short one who looks more native. That's not much of a description, but it's not my worry, so por que sudar? Oh, wait, they did say the big one wears a big planter's hat.''

Captain Gringo cut in. "We'll keep an eye out for them, Amigo. Meanwhile let's finish up here and see that skipper poco tiempo, right?''

Gaston seemed to have lost his appetite for more beans and rice, too. So they finished their cerveza, left a tip for the waitress they'd paid COD on the plank table, and got the hell out of there.

Gaston didn't ask why they were walking north along the quay instead of south toward the banana boat until they were far enough from the cantina for him to hand Captain Gringo stolen property and say, "You'd better put this on. That blond hair of yours stands out like the sore thumb. Mais, thank God you lost that other hat somewhere in your travels!''

Captain Gringo took the billed seaman's cap from Gaston and tried it on for size as he said, ''Good thinking. Where'd you swipe it, and how come I didn't notice?''

''Merde alors, if I'd been clumsy enough to let *you* see me take it très casual from its hook, the sailor who *hung* it there might have seen it as well, non? Eh bien, you do look more like a species of beached whale with that adorable new chapeau. Are we going anywhere in particular, Dick? I told you there are no practique trails inland from here.''

''Let's eat this apple one bite at a time. I just now figured what cost me my last hat. That wasn't a wild animal I met in that alley last night. I feel pretty sick about it, too. I decked a poor tarred-and-feathered guy who was only running away from a firing squad! I thought he was an *it,* and took all his wild sound and fury for an attack, when all the time he was just . . . Jesus, I think I'm going to puke!''

''Don't,'' warned Gaston, adding, ''That breakfast tasted bad enough going the other way. It wasn't your fault, Dick. They were going to catch him in any case. He was obviously in great pain as well. So you may have helped him in a way, by knocking him out, non?''

''Some help. That waitress said they buried him alive! She didn't say if he was awake or not at the time. Did you ever get the feeling a mother-fucker called Don Nogales might be a mother-fucker, Gaston?''

The Frenchman shrugged and said, ''It goes with the job of provincial governor. Since it is obvious the odd name of this seaport derives from the odd name of the adorable warlord's family, it is obvious they have been running things here très rough for some time. No doubt practice makes perfect, hein?''

''God damn it, how was I to know that big black fuzzy booger was a guy covered with tar and feathers? I never heard of anyone getting tarred and feathered this far south of Texas. That fucking Don Nogales *owes* me, Gaston!''

They were passing what looked like a big private steam yacht tied up to the quay, and there were people lounging

under an awning on the poop. So neither said anything until
they'd passed. Then Gaston said, "Forget it, Dick. You could
not have saved the poor devil even had you known he was not
a devil. His revolution ended for him well before you put him
out of his misery. To tar-and-feather a naked man takes more
out of him than the jokes would have it. Two out of three
such victims die of their burns not half as comfortably as the
one who was lucky enough to run into you."

"Yeah, I know. I've never thought it was funny, either. But
I still feel shitty and—"

"Stop feeling shitty and tell me what we do *now*!" Gaston
sighed, not bothering to point at the squad of soldiers farther
along the quay, coming their way.

Captain Gringo had eyes. He said, "Oboy, for openers,
about-face cool and casual—like we forgot something, right?"

The two soldiers of fortune stopped, faced each other, and
Gaston made a grand gesture back toward the cantina. Captain Gringo waited long enough to look like he was being
argued into it. Then they both started legging south, just a
little faster than they judged the soldiers had been marching.

It didn't work. They both saw the larger patrol lined up in
front of the hotel they'd left without checking out of a short
time ago. So they couldn't go back there, but they had to go
somewhere!

There was a gangplank lowered between the private yacht
they'd just passed and the quay. Captain Gringo muttered,
"Let me do the talking as we board that tub, Gaston."

"Merde alors, what can one say at such a time?"

"That's why I'd better do the talking. Slow down. We're
keeping an appointment, see?"

"Mais non, but this quay is getting too crowded, so, as
you say, what the hell, hein?"

There was nobody posted by the gangplank. But it was in
plain view of the poop. So the two soldiers of fortune were
uncomfortably aware of the curious eyes watching them as
they moved up it trying to look innocent. The squad coming
down from the north was so close now, they could hear
hobnails on cobbles behind them. Captain Gringo waved
casually at nobody in particular aboard, to make it seem they

were expected. Nobody waved back. But the soldiers marched by without stopping, so they were at least out of the frying pan—and the fire didn't look too bad yet.

Once his own eyes were shielded under the awning, too, Captain Gringo could see that the dozen-odd people lounging on the poop included four female figures dressed more Gibson girl than Hispanic. Most of the men wore tropic linen suits and straw hats, save for a couple of guys wearing seaman's caps and one guy under an imposing pith helmet. Before Captain Gringo could say anything, Pith Helmet asked, "Are you the guides Breslin sent?"

It was just as well. Up until that moment Captain Gringo had had no idea how he was to explain their spontaneous visit. He smiled innocently and said, "We heard you were looking for guides, Sir. To tell you the truth, we never heard of anyone called Breslin."

Pith Helmet frowned thoughtfully and said, "Good Lord, this is supposed to be a secret expedition, and you mean to tell me word has already gotten about? We've barely arrived, damn it!"

Captain Gringo said something about hearing about it from a friend of a friend as he stared over Pith Helmet's shoulder, south. From here he had a dismal view down the quay as far as the banana boat that wouldn't work either. The son-of-a-bitching soldiers were moving north—slowly so far, and thank God. The officer in charge seemed to be asking questions at each door they came to on the landward side.

Pith Helmet turned to one of the crew members—who'd been staring at Captain Gringo thoughtfully but poker-faced—and said, "You said your man Breslin would be waiting for us here this morning, Hardiman. These gentlemen say everyone in town knows why we've come. So where in the devil could your Breslin be?"

Hardiman shrugged and said, "I told you I sent a crewman ashore at daybreak to fetch him, Professor Slade. He wasn't home. But, like I said, he answered the cable we sent him from British Honduras. So he has to know you're in the market for jungle guides. If these guys know we've put in here, how long can it take Breslin to find out? The whole town's just a spit and a holler from here, right?''

Captain Gringo had to say something. The soldiers were getting closer. So he said, ''Maybe you guys hadn't heard. They had a revolution or something last night. Could this Breslin guy of yours have been mixed up in it?''

Hardiman laughed incredulously and said, ''Old Brez mixed up in greaser politics? Not hardly. He's an Indian trader, not a maniac. If you guys have been on the beach down here long enough to matter, you know that, once the shooting starts, it's open season in bananaland on anyone with blue eyes.''

Captain Gringo nodded, laughed back innocently, and said, ''That's why we're willing to work so cheap. Last night they were tarring and feathering guys before they shot 'em; and, like you say, we don't have powerful relatives in this neck of the woods. You say you're in the market for guides?''

Hardiman pointed at the professor with his chin and replied, ''These people are. I'm not about to stick my neck in that unexplored jungle to the west. If you know your way around in all that soggy spinach, how come you both seem to be breathing this morning?''

''We've run through the woods all up and down the Mosquito Coast. If it's so impossible, how come your mysterious trader Breslin has guides to offer?''

Hardiman shrugged and said, ''That's different. Breslin's boys are natives. The Mosquitos—Mosquito Indians, not bugs—don't put a reed arrow in brown skin as quick. White guides in Mosquito country are a contradiction in terms. I have it from Breslin personally. He's never dared to go to some of the villages he trades with.''

The soldiers on the quay were ominously closer now. Captain Gringo kept his voice desperately casual as he said, ''I'm starting to wonder about your contact's nerves, too. What are you people going to do if it turns out he and his native guides have left town for their health?''

Hardiman didn't answer. Professor Slade said, ''Damn it, we *have* to have guides! We're behind schedule as it is, and if that damned Grimsby expedition catches up with us still sitting here like frogs on a log . . .''

One of the women, who'd been trying to listen from her folding chair near the taffrail, gave up, stood up, and came over to join them. As she did so, Captain Gringo saw she was an attractive albeit middle-aged woman with silver-streaked black hair. Her tan pongee tropic blouse and skirt were practical. Her corset wasn't, if she meant to walk a mile in the tropics, in or out of a jungle. She hooked her arm through the professor's and asked, "Problems, Huggy Bear?"

Professor Slade, who looked nothing like a huggy bear to Captain Gringo, patted her hand and said, "Nothing I can't handle, Preshy." Then he introduced her to them as his wife, Elvira, which sounded a little less silly.

Despite the way she talked, old Elvira seemed to have more brains than her huggy bear, which only stood to reason. She said, "Well, if you want my opinion, Huggy Bear, those native boys are either coming or else they're not. Why don't we all just sit down and wait a bit? Meanwhile, we can interview these other gentlemen regarding their qualifications, see?"

Her huggy bear frowned thoughtfully. Then it seemed to sink in, and not a moment too soon. The two soldiers of fortune had just sat down after being introduced to the junior members of whatever-the-hell-this-was when the troops on the quay crunched to a halt and a wilted-looking officer trying to look dapper came aboard.

Hardiman, obviously the only old tropic hand present who wanted to admit being one, got between his passengers and the Honduran lieutenant to do the talking, in Spanish. The expedition members, all American from their accents, looked bemused as they tried to follow the conversation. Captain Gringo and Gaston followed it with no trouble at all, but tried to look bemused too as the officer told Hardiman, "We are making a routine search for a pair of dangerous guerrilla leaders, Señor Hardiman. You have heard, of course, of the trouble we had here only last night?"

Hardiman nodded soberly and replied, "Of course. Heard you won as usual. They never seem to learn how easy it is for Don Nogales to slip a few informers into any opposition party, eh?"

"Es verdad, but this last batch of rebels will not do that again. Our informers also told us to be on the lookout for a pair of professionals the rebels were expecting. Alas, we moved in a bit early. And it looks like it is going to be a hot day for beating bushes, too!"

Hardiman chuckled and asked if he'd like a drink. The lieutenant sighed and said, "Not on duty, gracias. Would it offend you if I were to ask you a little about your passenger list, Captain?"

"Not at all. The people you see over my shoulder are it. A Yanqui professor of antiquities and, of course, his helpers. They have a license from your central government to dig for lost cities in the jungles to the west."

"En verdad? There are no lost cities in the jungle to the west, Señor."

"You know that and I know that; but they wish to look for them anyway, and your government sees no harm in it. We were talking about some more dangerous strangers in these parts?"

"Ah, si, the notorious Ricardo Walker, better known as Captain Gringo, and that crazy little Legion deserter he runs wild with. I have never seen a picture of either, but we have a very good description and—"

Hardiman cut in with a laugh and said, "That's a funny picture you just painted, Lieutenant. My passengers would piss their pants if anyone like Captain Gringo got anywhere near them!"

"You know him on sight, Captain Hardiman?"

"Sure. Met him in Limón one time. He's about seven feet tall and looks just like what he is, a homicidal maniac. If he's anywhere near Puerto Nogales, don't worry. You're sure to spot him. Just look for a giant with bushy blond hair and a little hairy dark fiend who looks like . . . well, a fiend."

The lieutenant said he sure would, and went back ashore to march his patrol on up the quay as he relayed the grotesque but not totally inaccurate description to his noncoms.

Captain Gringo stared thoughtfully at Hardiman as a native messboy served gin and tonics all around. Hardiman refused to meet his eyes. Ergo, Hardiman knew. So what was

Hardiman's angle? Captain Gringo had never met the guy before. He shot a quizzical glance at Gaston. Gaston shook his head just enough to tell Captain Gringo he'd never met Hardiman before, either.

Professor Slade was one of those men who, though perhaps not so stupid as he seemed, could only think on one track at a time. Now that his wife had him considering the two soldiers of fortune as prospective guides, the old guy's questions were sensible enough. So Captain Gringo answered them as sensibly and truthfully as a guy applying for a job usually did. He said he knew how to navigate under the forest canopy, seldom stepped on a man-eating log, and got along as well as could be expected with most Indians one was apt to encounter in these parts. When he said he knew a few soothing words in the Mosquito dialect, Slade asked, "Do you know any Yumil Quax-ob?"

Captain Gringo shook his head and said, "That's not a language, Professor. It's Quiche, or what you'd probably call Maya, for the lords of the forest, the elder gods, or, in other words, spooks. We're a little far south for Maya religious practices."

He took a sip from his glass before adding, "Just as well. Some of that old time religion could get a little grim."

One of the women in the party, a petite redhead he'd been introduced to as a Miss O'Connor, maybe, leaned forward to ask breathlessly, "Is it true the Maya used to sacrifice virgins to their savage gods, Mister . . . ah?"

"Travis, Dick Travis, Ma'am," he lied, adding: "I wouldn't know about the virtue of the victims. But they sure went in for wholesale slaughter when the corn wasn't growing fast enough to please them. Fortunately, most Quiche have been converted to half-baked Christians by now, and, like I said, there aren't many, if any, this far south."

Professor Slade said, "We've been given to understand that Central America, not Mexico, was where the Maya culture began. We know they seem to have migrated north about three hundred A.D. We're not looking for *living* Maya. We're looking for the lost city of Cealcoquin."

Captain Gringo had never heard of the place. But Gaston

laughed and said, "Eh bien, which Cealcoquin would you prefer, Professor? Among the unwashed Honduran tribes, the name is as common for a village as Santa Maria is among those who wear shoes more regularly!"

Everyone but Professor Slade looked a little dismayed by this. Professor Slade simply said, "We want you to guide us to the *original* Cealcoquin, of course. It's a *city*, not a village. There should be a temple devoted to a white moon goddess and—"

"There should be seven cities of gold and a lake of El Dorado, too," Gaston cut in, adding: "I know the legend of La Madre Blanca, Professor. Some confused Honduran Indians still burn candles to her when the Catholic priests are not watching. But they are playing once-upon-a-time, hein?"

"All legends, in the end, are based on fact," said Slade firmly.

Gaston shrugged and replied, "Mais oui, anyone can see that at some time or another, a boy named Jacques must have climbed a beanstalk. I can show you all the beanstalks you would ever wish to see in those très fatigué woods to the west, Professor. But lost cities are another matter. Honduras derives its name from the Spanish, and translates roughly as 'getting in beyond one's depth,' a great void, a lot of nothing much, hein?"

He took a sip of gin and tonic, then added, "Central America is bigger than it looks on the map. One could lose Paris, easily, in the Honduran backwoods. Give those beanstalks over a thousand years to cover it, and you could stroll down the Champs Élysées without ever knowing it was there!"

Slade sniffed and said, "We don't intend to excavate the ruins. We only have to put them on film."

Captain Gringo perked up. He still had no intention of leading this pack of greenhorns anywhere, but as long as he was enjoying their shade and booze, it wouldn't hurt to be polite. So he said, "I didn't know this was a photographic expedition, Professor."

Slade said, "It's more than a photographic expedition. We

intend to take the first Kinetoscopic views of the lost Honduran civilization.''

Captain Gringo laughed incredulously and asked, "Are we talking about those new moving pictures, Professor?"

"Of course. What else would 'Kinetoscope' mean? As a matter of fact, we have two Edison cameras, a projector to edit the film as we go, and of course all the film and darkroom equipment we can possibly carry along."

Hardiman must have been waiting his chance. Before Captain Gringo could come up with a polite reply to such a wild statement, the skipper caught his eye and said, "Let me show you the load you guys will have to deal with, ah, Travis. It's up forward and we, ah... have *other* things to talk about."

That was what Captain Gringo had been afraid of. He rose, excused himself from the company on the poop, and followed the more worldly-looking Hardiman forward along the off-shore rail. As soon as they were out of earshot, he asked Hardiman, "Do you have any smokes on you? I've been trying to buy some cigars since last evening, and it's gotten complicated as hell."

Hardiman reached into his jacket and took out a couple of claros, but said, "Don't light up just yet. I hate noise."

He opened a stateroom door as Captain Gringo put the cigars away with a nod of thanks. They stepped inside and the skipper switched on the overhead light, saying, "There's even more bang-bang in the hold. But we'd best see how you do with what's here, for now."

Captain Gringo stared soberly at the piled equipment almost filling the compartment. He could see that a little more than half of it consisted of photographic gear and camping supplies, which made sense. But he couldn't help wondering what a moving-picture expedition was doing with a Maxim machine gun, two cases of repeating Krag rifles, and all that ammo. So he asked.

Hardiman said, "As you may have guessed, it takes more than the usual charter fees to keep this tub operating at a decent profit. As long as I was bringing those greenhorns up the coast, I figured to... well, run a few guns."

"Don't you mean you're using the professor and his bunch as a cover for your gun-running, Hardiman?"

Hardiman laughed easily and said, "Look, let's not spar around. You know what I am and I know what you are. I figured out who you were about the time those soldados asked me about the notorious Captain Gringo. I figured you were more use to us alive than you would be to them dead."

"Oh shit, I thought you were hot for my ass. But, okay, I like you too. What's the pitch?"

Hardiman said, "I'm working on one, playing by ear. The original plan was to use the professor's government permit as an excuse to land a few more guns than a sensible expedition might need, see?"

"That's for sure. Even wild Indians don't come at anybody wild enough to need more than one repeating weapon per expedition member. Didn't they ask you about that machine gun?"

"Sure. I told 'em some wild Indians down here are *really* wild. You know how greenhorns are. Forget about them. They're just a smokescreen in case any Honduran customs guys get nosy. Let's talk about us. What the fuck's going on up here in Puerto Nogales? The guys who were supposed to take these weapons and all the ammo in the hold have vanished on me."

Captain Gringo shrugged and said, "If they vanished right, they may contact you when things simmer down. If they got rounded up with the other rebels, you can kiss 'em adios for keeps. The local military command plays sort of rough."

Hardiman grimaced and said, "Shit, we sell guns and ammo to rebels. We're not dumb enough to fight beside them. My dealer here is a licensed Indian trader named Breslin. I tell the truth when I can. Saves a lot of strain on the brain."

He took out a folded envelope and handed it over, saying, "If you can make it to any of his trading posts on this rough map with that machine gun, the Krags, and say half a ton of ammo, we'll be much obliged."

"I'm sure you would be. What's in it for Gaston and me?"

"Our undying gratitude. I just saved your ass, Walker. You want egg in your beer, too?"

Captain Gringo stared thoughtfully at the older knockaround guy and started to say something. Then he decided that if they couldn't see how easy it would be to double-cross them, there was no sense pointing it out. But Hardiman said, "You can't sell the stuff anywhere else in a jungle Breslin controls. If you take off from the expedition on your own, you'll have our Indians as well as the Honduran army to duck. By the way, how come they're after you in the first place, Walker? Didn't you and Gaston fight *for* Honduras just a few months back?"

Captain Gringo shrugged and said, "We fought for one faction against another. We're professionals, not patriots. I have to explain this shit to *you*, Hardiman?"

The gunrunner chuckled knowingly and said, "If the little brown bastards ever get tired of killing one another, we'll all be out of business. But they never will. So let's get back to getting my real cargo ashore and inland where it'll be on sale, at a modest price, next time the wind shifts. Do we have a deal?"

"Not one I like all that much. But you seem to have us by the short hairs. Don't you even want to offer us expense money, for God's sake?"

"Hey, I'm offering you your fucking asses, and the professor will probably pay you something for acting as his guides. So don't be ungrateful, Kid."

Captain Gringo asked, "What's he paying for a guided tour of lost Mayan cities this season?"

Hardiman shrugged and said, "You'll have to work it out with him. He paid me the going charter-boat rates and I kept it sort of vague how thick I was with his so-called travel agents. I know you'll eat good, and with four dames along, you ought to work in some slap-and-tickle. Two of the dames are actresses, and you know what they say about actresses, Kid."

"Never mind what they *say* about 'em. Why is the professor taking even *one* actress on a scientific expedition?"

"How the hell should I know? Did he ask me dumb questions about *my* business? Look, we gotta get back so you can make a deal with him before that little French asshole convinces them they're on a wild-goose chase.''

As they stepped back out on deck, Captain Gringo couldn't help observing, ''That's just what it is, you know. Where the hell are we supposed to lead them, and who gets to carry the gear and swing the mâchetes?''

Hardiman locked the stateroom door and soothed, ''Look, it don't matter where you lead 'em, as long as you lead 'em to one of our trading posts where you can drop off the guns and ammo. As for porters, you can hire all you like right here in town, now that the army has you all down as a mess of harmless jerk-offs with a government license to hunt lost cities. Jesus, Walker, haven't you ever taken advantage of greenhorns before?''

''Not as often as you have, I imagine. But I'm learning.''

They went aft to rejoin the others, just in time. Gaston was holding forth on the legend of the white moon goddess of Honduras, making it sound like the fairy tale it probably was as he continued, ''So then, boys and girls, the beautiful white lady finished her three-sided pyramid and, no doubt with some fatigue, since she was supposed to be a virgin, she produced three sons who, naturally, were also gods and, even more alarming, full-grown at birth.''

He broke off when Captain Gringo sat down again, lighting a cigar and shooting the old Frenchman a warning look as he announced, ''Well, now that I've seen what has to be packed in, we'd better talk about getting some native help, Professor. I'd say we need at least thirty peones, and the peones, of course, will say they want to bring their women along.''

Slade said, ''That's ridiculous,'' and Captain Gringo said, ''I know. But you can't even get an army to march without feminine companionship down here; and, no offense, if you guys mean to take these four ladies along, there's just no way you're going to get celibate porters.''

The professor's wife laughed. Miss O'Connor giggled. The other two looked sort of indignant, and one snapped, ''I'll have you know I'm not that kind of a girl, Sir!''

She didn't say what any of the other women were, and it would have been sophomoric to say three out of four wasn't bad. So he smiled and soothed, "If we don't make moral judgments about the natives, they won't make any about us. The mujeres tagging along will expect to be fed, but they won't demand pay. The men will expect about ten cents a day, U.S., along with all they can eat. They can't eat as much as we do. They're not used to it. Can do, Professor?"

Slade looked relieved and replied, "Oh, that's much more reasonable than I was led to expect. They told me porters would cost me a dollar a day."

Captain Gringo didn't look up at Hardiman, who was looking down at him as if he were awfully stupid. Captain Gringo told the expedition leader, "Gaston and me will cost you more than a dollar a day. How does five a day, each, strike you?"

Slade grimaced and said, "A bit steep, if you must know. Damned few executives make thirty-five dollars a week back in the States right now!"

"We're not back in the States, Professor. You're not hiring executives, either. You need experienced jungle hands who can keep you alive in a green hell you frankly have no business entering. I'd best say right off, it may not be easy. You'd be safer if you had a dozen guys like us coming along. But for ten bucks a day you're getting two, and that's better than none. The other hired help will run you three or four bucks more. So add it up and you're fielding your expedition for less than fifteen bucks a day. If you can't afford that, you've got no business wandering about in the Honduran jungles. But feel free to try, if you want to try it on your own."

Elvira Slade nudged her husband and said, "Let's not dicker, Huggy Bear. The young man's already saving us a fortune on those porters they said would be waiting for us here."

Slade brightened and said, "By Jove, that's true!" adding in a fond aside to Captain Gringo, "She's better at figures than I am. I agree to your terms, Travis. How soon can we get started?"

Captain Gringo glanced over at the now deserted quay simmering in the sun more seriously now that the morning haze had burned off, and said, "With luck, we can recruit some help before La Siesta sets in. But there's no way we can get them started before La Siesta is over, around three-thirty this afternoon. The sun will set around six. The moon's been setting just before midnight the last few nights. So, let's say we manage to move out around five or six, we should just about be clearing the corn milpas outside of town about the time we have to make our first campfire."

Slade frowned and said, "My God, we can't afford to waste a whole day just getting started! I told you a rival expedition is out to photograph the same blasted scenery!"

Captain Gringo nodded, but said, "You just hired yourself some old tropic hands, Professor. So take some advice about the tropics. The first rule down here is *take it easy*! If you think Gaston and me move slower than you're used to moving, wait until you see the guys we hope to hire. And when you see them, let *us* give the orders. Europeans and North Americans just confuse them, shouting at them to get the lead out. Tropic natives aren't as lazy as they look and even act. They grow three crops a year to our farmers' one. But you have to let 'em do it their own way, and their way doesn't include dropping dead of heat stroke. I don't want any of you people suffering heat stroke, either. So, Numero Uno, when *we* go ashore, *you* guys and gals stay aboard no matter how bored you get. You won't find any quaint native shops open, and if you see any quaint natives dancing quaintly under that sun out there, shoot 'em. They have to have rabies. It's not as hot under this awning right now as it's going to get before it gets cooler. By noon, rays you may not feel will be coming through that canvas. So take a tip from the quaint natives and lie down in your staterooms between twelve and three. With your duds off, whether you can sleep or not. When we do move out, you'll find your legs weaker than you expect. Until you're used to it, this climate can tire you out just looking at you."

Everyone but Professor Slade looked impressed. He said, "That's all very well for you to say, but my rival, Grimsby—"

"Is a human being, even as you and I," Captain Gringo

cut in, adding with a reassuring smile: "Let's hope he *does* work like a beaver to beat you, Professor. If nobody was waiting here to meet you, nobody will be waiting for this Grimsby guy, and you just hired the best in town. If his ship comes in two minutes from now, there's just no way he's going to beat you into the jungle tonight. So if it does while we're gone, for Pete's sake don't try to *do* anything about it before we get back. I'm willing to *lead* you through the jungle. I'm not about to *carry* you!"

Elvira Slade said her husband understood. Which meant she did, at least. So Captain Gringo rose and muttered, "Come on, Gaston. We've got some business to attend to before it gets too hot."

Gaston said nothing until the two of them were moving along the quay together toward the center of town again. Then he squinted south and muttered, "That banana boat has left, I see. No matter, I am sure we can find a coastal schooner now that the army has wandered off somewhere."

"I know where the army is. It's in the shade, acting sensible. You were wrong about that hotel, but the whores you recruited last night were okay. How do we go about recruiting, say, two or three dozen porters?"

Gaston looked dismayed and asked, "Are you serious? I meant what I said about lost cities, Dick. There are no ruins within très fatigué days of here, and when one *does* encounter a few old piles of weed-covered rock in the higher country to the west, they are not lost. Most of the interesting ones are on the survey maps and, by the way, the army carries those same survey maps!"

"Will you calm down about the stupid army? They're not looking for us. They're looking for a couple of notorious soldiers of fortune. We're with a licensed asshole expedition of some kind if anybody asks, see?"

"Believe me, my budding motion-picture actor, they shall surely ask! And if our fake ID fails to match the names they have down as licensed explorers—"

"Jesus, what a worrywart," Captain Gringo cut in, explaining, "Look, did that officer ask for us by the names on our spanking-new identification papers? He told Hardiman he was looking for a Captain Gringo Walker, not an innocent tourist called Ricardo Travis, remember?''

"Oui, I remember whoever betrayed the rebels we were to contact told the army we were expected in this part of the universe as well! So why are we walking right back into town, Dick?''

"Because we're a couple of purloined letters, Dummy! You saw how they never even asked to see our papers when Hardiman vouched for us back there. We all look alike to them. As long as we stay attached to what they dismiss as an expedition of harmless idiots, we have a perfect cover. So let's stay attached to it, right?''

"Merde alors, you are right about them being idiots. I am not sure how dangerous leading nine men and four women into unexplored jungle may be.''

"Don't tell any of them the jungles to the west are unexplored. We're supposed to be guides who know where we're *going*, remember?''

Since the checkout time at the hotel they'd spent the night in was noon, and since it wasn't noon yet, they might have been tempted to just go back there and use it as their base of operations. But since they were used to living on the run, they didn't. Gaston remembered a posada up a side street. The upstairs rooms had neither mosquito netting nor running water, but since they wouldn't be spending the night there, what the hell.

They'd left their travel kits aboard the chartered yacht. But the landlady didn't ask about luggage or even ask them to sign in, once she'd been paid off by her old amigo, Gaston Someone-She'd-Seen-Before. She just handed them a couple of keys and went back to her quarters to undress for La Siesta and a nice young lad she'd taken on to teach the posada business to, when business wasn't so slow.

Like most native inns, this one's lower story was a semi-cantina—about to close for La Siesta unless someone came in for drinks poco tiempo. Captain Gringo bought a fistful of claro cigars as well as a bottle of Madeira. Gaston had said it might take him awhile to scout up the hired help they'd need. So Captain Gringo was smoking and drinking alone in the darkest corner when, of all people, the waitress from the cantina closer to their first hotel came in looking hot and tired as she fanned as much of her chest as she could decently show over the top of her low-cut blouse.

He was hoping she'd go on upstairs without spotting him. He still liked girls, and she was prettier than either of the bums he'd spent the night with. But she worked too close to the main drag for comfort and she'd already proven she liked to gossip.

But she saw him, smiled in surprise, and moved over to join him as he rose, managed to smile back, and asked, "Just get off, Inez?"

She sighed and said, "Not exactly. I just quit for good. Do you know what that brute of a manager expected of me, after making me work like a dog since the wee small hours, Ricardo?"

As they both sat down, Captain Gringo slid the only glass across to her, half-filled, and said, "I can imagine. I think you're pretty, too."

She picked up the Madeira, gulped it down like spring water, and gasped, "Oh, that feels good going down! May I have some more, por favor?"

He refilled the glass but said, "You know your own capacity better than anyone else, Inez. But Madeira's stronger than sangria, in case you're not used to it."

She said, "Right now I could drink the ocean dry, salt and all! It is not as hot in here. But outside, the trades are barely blowing and . . . by the way, how did you know I was staying here, Ricardo?"

"I was born sneaky. Let's see if I can get us an extra glass."

She shook her head and said, "Don't bother. I do not mind touching my lips to the same glass as your own, if *you* don't mind, that is."

He raised an eyebrow and replied, "You don't have lips.

Those are rose petals, I'm sure." So she fluttered her lashes coyly and raised the glass again to kiss the rim suggestively as he wondered, vaguely, how far he wanted to carry this romantic bullshit.

She must have wondered too. She said, "I am glad you were smart enough to find your way here, Ricardo. Would it offend you to hear I was a little cross with you when I did not find you waiting for me near that cantina? I thought you had only been flirting with me earlier."

"Well, it crossed my mind you might only be killing time that way, too. That's why I didn't ask your room number when I checked in upstairs just now."

She blinked and asked, "You checked in? You have your own room here?"

"Well, I had to say *something* to the patrona. Don't worry, I wasn't taking anything for granted, like your boss."

She wrinkled her pert brown nose and said, "Pooh, he is old and fat. I would not wish for to spend La Siesta with him even if I did not have a handsome Yanqui of my own to come home to!"

That was about as open an invitation as he was likely to get, and he knew she was going to be mad as hell if he tried not to understand it.

If there was one thing he didn't want Inez to be, it was mad at him. She was the only person for blocks who'd heard him say he was off that banana boat, not attached to an expedition. So he reached across the table, took her soft, smaller hand in his, and asked, "Now that you've come home to me, what are we doing in this ridiculous upright position, Querida?"

She squeezed back and murmured, "We must be discreet. I have my good name to consider. Which room have you taken? If I were to go on up ahead of you, innocently . . ."

He nodded and slid the key across to her, saying, "Numero cinco, near the corner. Five minutes?"

She palmed the key and murmured, "Bring the bottle, and if it's more than three, I may start without you!"

Then she rose, bade him good afternoon in a louder, less informal tone, and headed for the stairs. She hadn't been walking that way when she came in. But then she hadn't had anyone to wag her ass like that at, out under the hot tropic sun.

He chuckled, took a drag on his smoke, and poured another casual drink as he risked a sidelong glance at the bar. The barkeep had his back turned to him and was reading a newspaper. So what the hell was he doing down here?

He rose silently as possible, taking the bottle along as he moved toward the stairwell. When he got there, the barkeep didn't bother to turn his head, but murmured softly, "Careful, Yanqui. She has more than one admirer."

Captain Gringo sighed and asked, "Are you one of them, Amigo?"

The barkeep chuckled, and his voice stayed friendly as he replied, "No, thank God. I'm not in shape for that much fighting. You may get away with it in your own room. I would have had to stop you had you tried to go to *hers*. Our Inez is very hard on the furniture. But you are on another wing of the building, so go with God but try to be discreet, eh?"

"If I had the brains of a gnat, I'd head for the front door instead. But I have to wait here until my comrade returns. Could I buy you a drink before I go on up?"

"You paid for that bottle, Amigo, and I sell nothing else here. If your little Frenchman was not an old amigo of La Patrona I would not have offered so much advice unrequested, eh?"

"I understand. I'm sorry I insulted your honor, Señor."

"Esta nada, one gets used to being taken for a pimp, working behind a bar. It's been nice talking to you, but I have to see about closing now."

Captain Gringo went on upstairs. The hallway was pretty dark, even at midday, since there were no windows unshuttered or lamps lit when it was this hot. He groped his way to a door with a big blue 5 painted on it and naturally found the latch unlocked for him. So he had to go on in before he could be surprised, a little, to find Inez already undressed, reclining across the bed cover with a pillow wadded under her shapely hips. The nicest surprise was that she was built even nicer than expected, once she'd shed that loose peasant blouse and pleated skirt.

He locked the door behind him, moved over to the bed, and got rid of the bottle as he took her in his arms. She kissed back passionately and moved one of his hands down between her brown thighs to prove to him she was really a girl. As he politely explored her fuzzy gates of paradise, she gasped, "Prisa! For why are you teasing me so? For why don't you take *your* clothes off, Querido?"

That sounded like a hell of a good idea. So he let go, and as she rolled over, giggling, to lie on the pillow with her derrière thrust up at him invitingly, he shucked his duds poco tiempo, letting everything fall anywhere it wanted to save for the gun rig that he shoved prudently under the mattress, near the head. Then he got on her tail, entering her dog-style and apparently by surprise, since she gleeped like a goosed schoolgirl and gasped, "Oh my God, I did not know you stood so tall!"

"Am I hurting you?" he asked, withdrawing halfway. She arched her spine to take it deeper as she protested, "Not at all. I love surprises. But hurry and come that way so we can get romantic, eh?"

He laughed, withdrew, and turned her on her back to enter her that way, asking, "Is this more romantic, Querida?"

She replied by raising her legs impossibly, locking her bare ankles around the nape of his neck, and hugging him down against her firm, tawny breasts to kiss him—more lusty than romantic, but it did feel better this way. So they both went deliriously mad for a while. And while the heat, even indoors, made for sweaty rutting indeed, Inez seemed a born sweaty-rutter, a girl a man could let himself get as piggy with as he wanted to. So he did.

She came twice that way to his once, or said she did. Then she wanted to get on top, explaining it might be cooler that way. It wasn't. There was nothing cool about the way the cantina girl made love. A little bell rang deep in Captain Gringo's brain as he couldn't help wondering if she was going to disappoint him, in the end, by mentioning payment for such grand services rendered. But meanwhile, she moved her here-and-now marvelously. So he just had to lie back and enjoy it as she slid her lust-flushed interior up and down his shaft. Had it really been only six or eight hours since the last time he'd been treated so nicely by a lady? He gave up trying to add up the hours since the last time he'd come in Floralinda, or maybe it had been Rosalita, bless them both. But as he counted the ways Evita could charm, he found himself wondering why he cared whatever had become of those other whores since he and Gaston had snuck out on them in the cold, gray dawn.

He decided it was unfair to compare Inez to the whores when she suddenly collapsed atop him limply and moaned, "Oh, I am so filled with happy feelings I can't stand it. But don't take it out. Don't ever take it out."

He wasn't about to. He was almost there himself. He rolled her onto her back again to move it in her right as she lay spread-eagled and submissive, crooning, "Do it, do it, do it! But forgive me if I cannot move with you right now! I am weak with love, Ricardo. You are too much hombre for poor little me. You must have been at sea a long time, no?"

He was too hot to lose interest all the way. But as he went on making love to her, he cursed her memory under his breath. He didn't want her yakking about her Yanqui boyfriend off a banana boat, now. So how was he going to keep her from doing so unless he kept her here in bed until it was time to leave town?

The answer seemed obvious enough as he suddenly peaked and pounded her to sobbing glory. But once he'd ejaculated in her, hard, he could tell he'd never be up to much jungle-hiking after a whole afternoon of *this* great exercise!

She'd been pleading for mercy even before he came in her. So he kissed her fondly, rolled off, and fumbled on the floor for a smoke and a light. Inez leaned across him, brushing his naked back with her moist nipples as she got the bottle and rolled back with it, pressing it to her thirsty lips. He had trouble finding the damned matches, since they'd fallen out of a pocket. But in the end they wound up propped against the bedboard, with a claro between his teeth and the bottle cradled between her breasts as if she were nursing it. She heaved a sigh and said, "Oh, this feels so domestico, as if we were married, no?"

"Don't talk dirty. We both enjoy sex too much to even think of such a disgusting way of life!"

She giggled and said, "Si, but I enjoy fantasy, between sailors. Have some of this wine, Querido. As soon as we cool off a bit, I intend to get you most hot again."

He laughed, took another drag on the claro, and said, "You finish it. If I'd known what Fate had in store for me this afternoon, I wouldn't have drunk as much of that strong stuff as I did, uh, waiting for you."

"Oh, go ahead," she insisted, holding the bottle up to him as she added: "I have had more to drink than you, and it just makes me feel like making love."

He shook his head and said, "No thanks. I really mean it. You girls don't know how booze can let a man down, you lucky little things."

"Oh come on, get hot with me, Ricardo."

"Have I been treating you *coldly*, Doll Box? I don't *dare* drink any more if we're spending the whole siesta together like this. It's . . . let's see, not even two yet, and we haven't gotten around to half the positions. Just let me finish this smoke and . . . humm, there must be *some* position left in bed. Maybe against the wall? Oh, right, we haven't done it Chinese Duck style yet."

"Are you mocking me?" she asked in a suddenly sullen voice. Something went *Boinggg!* in his skull where he filed his memories. He said, "Hey, you've had enough of that Madeira too, Doll Box"—before the same file drawer warned him that whatever one said to a surly drunk, that wasn't it.

She confirmed his judgment by snapping, "Don't you call me a drinker of too much Madeira, you know-it-all Yanqui! I'll tell you when I have had enough. Who do you think you are, my father?"

He snuffed out the claro, took the bottle away from her, and rolled her on her back again to kiss her before she could talk really nasty. She twisted her lips away and whimpered, "Don't! I cannot make love when I have been insulted. Why can't you brutes understand that, damn you all?"

He was beginning to see what the barkeep had meant. It was nice to know she wasn't a whore. But a crazy bitch wasn't really a great improvement.

He stopped trying and said, "All right, I'll stop being a brute if you will. I don't see a chessboard around here anywhere, but maybe we could kill some time just sleeping awhile. It would probably be a switch for both of us."

She lay under him, blinking her eyes as if she were confused about just where she was. Then she placed a palm atop his bare buttock and pulled him closer, saying, "Oh, go ahead. I don't mind, if you really have to."

"I don't really have to do anything, Inez. Forget it."

"Of course you do," she insisted, adding: "All men are alike once they are aroused. Go ahead and put it in so you can get it over with, eh?"

"Forget it," he growled, rolling off her to reach automatically for the bottle. But that was another dumb kid game, too. So he left the booze on the side table, didn't reach for another smoke either, and sat up to grope for his clothes on the floor between his bare feet.

Inez sobbed. "You are not leaving me now, after all we have been to one another?"

He grimaced and muttered, "Jesus, they must all read the same books." Then he reassured her. "Relax. I just want to see what time it is, if I can ever find my watch."

"You are angry with me! I can tell! Oh Querido, por favor do not be angry with me! Come, let us make love some more, eh?"

He found his pocket watch, saw it was after two but nowhere's near three, and put the watch on the bed table by the bottle, wondering how the hell he was going to last until Gaston got back with good or bad news. He was almost sure he'd have a screamer on his hands if he just got dressed and went back downstairs to wait.

He lit another smoke and swung his legs back aboard the mattress as Inez sobbed, "Oh, I was so afraid you were leaving! I do not know what makes me say bad things at times. Am I forgiven, Querido?"

"Sure, sure, just lie still and don't fight it. I'm not going anywhere because, for one thing, I got no place better to go."

"Let me prove my love for you!" she pleaded, plastering her naked and still moist body against his side as she reached for his flaccid, no-longer-virile member. He didn't argue as she toyed with him. It felt no better nor worse than pissing, and this cigar was fresher than the last one he'd smoked. He hooked his free arm over to cuddle her closer as she snuggled her head against his bare chest, murmuring dumb things about him being different and so understanding. He figured he probably was. The trouble with understanding women was that once you had a real bitch figured out, you couldn't figure out what you had wanted with her. A tame shrew made a dull pet, since they had so few other tricks to offer.

It didn't take a whole lot of brains for Inez to figure out that a man with a limp dong just wasn't in her power. It seemed to upset her. But she'd just found out he wouldn't play the usual games. So she started kissing her way down him as she skillfully stroked his limp shaft, which didn't feel quite so limp now.

He lay back, blowing smoke rings till she was blowing him good. He wondered how he was ever going to be able to keep it soft in such pleasant surroundings. Then he wondered why the hell he had to try. *That* was a kid game too. If a lady wanted to suck a gentleman off, the least he could do would be to let her, like the sport he was.

Inez detected his growing interest with her teasing lips and, as it grew more, tongue and tonsils. It seemed to inspire her to greater effort. She moved around until she was crouched over his groin with her knees folded under her between his shins. Her head moved great in that position, too. He'd have never lasted as long as he did had not he been overworking the old organ grinder lately. As he lay there, enjoying a good cigar while Inez smoked him, trying to inhale, he decided to really forgive her. She was beautiful as well as a bitch. So he put the cigar aside, cupped her bobbing head in his palms, and helped her move her head faster.

She giggled and murmured, with her mouth full, "Would you like for to fuck me again, Querido?"

That sounded fair. So he rolled her over on her back to mount her right again. He saw he'd made a tactical error when she smiled up at him triumphantly and said, "Hah! I *told* you no man could resist my pussy!"

He said, "When you're right, you're right," and just pretended she was Miss Ellen Terry or some other nicer lady in the *Police Gazette* as he simply used her pulsing vagina to jerk it off all the way.

His passion, though not directed so much at her as she thought, seemed to surprise and thus arouse Inez. She gasped, "Oh, I am coming again, even though I am annoyed with you, I think, I mean I thought, I mean just do it, do it, do it! I am almost there and, no, I ammmmmm!"

That made two of them. It felt so good he even kissed her as his overstimulated genitals managed a protracted, almost painful, orgasm they hadn't really needed. She took that as a compliment too, and crooned, "You bad boy, you really *do* need me, don't you?"

He said something polite and added, "I think you just knocked me out," as he rolled off to lie, eyes closed, on the edge where the sheets were dry and a little cooler. She asked if he wished for to go to sleep now. He said he sure did, and not to wake him before three unless the building caught on fire.

She said she was exhausted, too. But, as she kept moving around like a kitten digging for a place to shit, he opened one eye, saw she was getting dressed, and asked how come.

She said, "Go back to sleep, Querido. I shall be right back. There are things a discreet woman must do after making love. The things I need are naturally in my own room. I shall return before you wake, and if you don't wake up for me, I may fuck you in your sleep."

He smiled with his eyes closed and said he meant to hold her to that. She rose—as fully dressed as a sensible native girl ever got down here—and tiptoed out, shutting the door behind her.

Captain Gringo sat up and swung his feet to the floor. He checked the time. Too early, damn it. He got dressed anyway, leaving only his jacket and stolen seaman's cap on the bed table as he moved over to the window, hooking up his gun rig.

He opened the shutters and looked down. The window opened on a gap between the posada and the blank stucco wall of the building next door. From the weedy patch below, one could easily slip into the alley running behind the posada. He closed the shutters again. There were times one didn't need light on the subject, and it was hot as hell out there right now.

He moved to the bed again and fluffed up the pillows before drawing the thin topsheet over them. It didn't really look like a sleeping figure, once you studied it. But it might at first glance.

He checked the time again. No matter how you sliced it, Gaston just wasn't going to be back in less than half an hour, even if he came back at the end of La Siesta the way he'd been told to.

Captain Gringo moved over to the corner, on the far side of the door springs, and drew his .38, feeling a little overdramatic. He knew he could be wrong, and even if he was right, there was more than one way to play the rest of this scene out. Just running would have been the best way, if Gaston weren't due back here shortly.

A million years went by. His legs were getting tired for some reason. He hadn't walked that much lately. But just standing still could take a lot out of a man's legs, as many a soldier standing guard could tell you.

Another million years went by. It was starting to look as if he'd been wrong. He hoped he was wrong. Life would be a lot less complicated if he was wrong. But Captain Gringo was still alive because, in the past, he'd guessed right and, more important, gone with his hunch.

He fumbled out his watch with his free hand. Then he shook it. It had to have stopped. He had to have been standing here longer than that. He decided to count to a thousand and that would be it. Enough of this shit was enough. He counted to a thousand, slowly. Naturally, nothing had happened by then and he'd promised his legs he'd give up after counting to a thousand. But he started counting to two thousand, anyway.

He got to twelve hundred and forty-six before the door cracked open an inch and his heart skipped a beat. He held his breath as the door opened farther and Inez stepped in with her back to him.

He resisted the impulse to say "Boo!" For one thing, it could scare an innocent maiden half to death, and for another, innocent maidens didn't usually enter rooms so sneaky. As Inez slipped clear of the door, the broader back of a chino uniform materialized beside her, and even though he'd half expected it, Captain Gringo's heart still skipped another beat.

The cop whispered, "Are you sure he's asleep?"

Captain Gringo clubbed him across the back of the neck at the base of his skull and slammed the door shut as he growled, "I'm not. But he is."

Inez, of course, jumped halfway out of her skin and onto the bed in sheer terror. But to her credit, she didn't scream as she rolled over, staring up at him wide-eyed as he stepped over the cop he'd put on the floor. He pointed his gun muzzle at the wine bottle by the bed and said, "Drink it. All of it."

"Ricardo!" she gasped. "What is going on? I do not understand!"

He held the gun on her as he dropped to one knee to reach back and feel the side of the cop's throat, saying, "Sure you do. Never put cheap knockout drops in warm wine if you're not woman enough to drink it yourself. This cop you intended to share the reward with doesn't need knockout drops. Unless you want to wind up in the same condition, you'd better swallow the whole bottle, Baby!"

He rose to his full, somewhat alarming, height and said, "I mean it, Inez. If you'd tried to pull this shit on a lot of guys as nice as me, we wouldn't be having this conversation. I just put a full-grown man away for keeps. How hard do you think I'd have to smack *you* with this hunk of solid steel in my hand?"

"Please don't hurt me!" she whimpered, drawing up her legs and, as a natural afterthought, raising the hem of her skirt to expose her inviting lap of luxury. He snorted in annoyance and said, "I'm trying not to. But you sure aren't making it easy. That drugged wine should put you out for a good four hours. I only need three. So take your medicine like a good little girl, and when you wake up it'll all be over."

Inez reached for the bottle but pleaded, "I can't drink it all, Ricardo. Carlos there said one or two sips would knock you out for at least an hour."

He frowned down at her and said, "Let's see if I get this straight. Your boyfriend the cop couldn't have tailed me here. If he'd spotted me before you slipped out just now to inform on me, he wouldn't have wanted to share part of the reward on me. So, right, you spotted me, did your best to knock me out with stuff you naturally keep on hand for such emergencies, and when that wouldn't work, tried to screw me unconscious, for which I'll always be grateful. Drink up while I tell you what else I figured out, waiting behind that door."

She took a hesitant sip and protested, "Oh, it tastes so awful."

He said, "Yeah, smells even worse in a warm bottle in a stuffy room. Chloral hydrate's for rolling drunks, not undercover police work, Doll Box. But it was your choice, so you get to drink it. I mean *now,* poco tiempo! I haven't time to fuck around."

She took a healthier gulp, then batted her lashes at him some more and purred, "You didn't say that when we *were* fucking around, Ricardo."

"What can I tell you, it was puppy love? Keep drinking. Lucky for you, there's less than half a bottle left. But get it down, or I'll have to put you down another way."

She must not have wanted him to do that. She took a couple of serious gulps, and then, since the first she'd already downed was starting to lull her, shrugged in resignation and started swigging seriously as he growled, "That's a good girl. You took some time hunting down a particular cop. He came alone, like I sure was hoping he would. You want to tell me about that?"

She stared up at him, a little owlishly, and said, "Carlos said he did not think Captain Gringo would leave on that banana boat, as everyone else thought. Carlos said the reward posters said Captain Gringo was wanted for killing an army officer in Los Estados Unidos and that it would be madness for him to board a ship bound for New Orleans, see?''

"Carlos was smart as hell, up until a minute ago. The bit about the reward poster answers my question about how you two figured out who I was. So what we have here is a sordid little love quarrel between a known waterfront tramp and her policeman lover. Are you listening to any of this, Inez?''

"Si, I think so. But Carlos and me did not have any fight.''

"Sure you did. Just wait until you hear what the judge says, no matter how you tell it. Unless you're *smart*, of course. Are you a smart girl, Inez?''

"I used to think I was. Now you have me very confused, Ricardo. It was you who hit Carlos, not I. Why should they not believe me when I tell them?''

"Suspicious natures, I guess. If you don't play your cards just the way I tell you to, you'll wake up with a hangover and your known lover, killed with the proverbial blunt anything, on your hands. But we wouldn't want that to happen. So I'll tell you what you're going to do. Finish that sleepy juice while I tell you.''

"I don't wish for to drink any more. It is making me feel funny.''

"You'll feel funnier if they tar and feather you before they make you dig your own grave. If you don't drink it all, I won't tell you how to get away with murder in a town that plays so rough!''

She drank it all. She was crying when she lowered the bottle from her lips. He knew she wouldn't be paying attention for long. So he said, "Bueno. Numero Uno; this cop's lying dead in my room not yours. So, as soon as you wake up again, drag him over to the window and dump him outside so that when they find him it'll look like he was slugged by the usual people he chases, in the *alley*. They probably won't even question you or the people in this posada. If they do, just remember which room is your own and forget you were ever anywhere near this side of the building.''

She shook her head to clear it. But some of what he was

saying must have still been getting through. For she said, "I could never lift a man that size, damn you."

He said, "Try. It's much less work than digging your own grave. I'll help by leaving him propped up near the window for you before I leave. Don't scream when you wake up after dark to see a dead guy staring at you. It'll only be an old friend. I'll lock the two of you in as I leave. The door has a spring latch. So you simply have to get rid of the cop and go out to get laid."

"You . . . animal!"

"Takes one to know one, I suppose. But go get laid anyway. It's a much better alibi than saying you were in your room reading the Bible when they get around to finding a dead cop in a nearby alley."

She suddenly fell back, saying, "Wheeee! I wish for to get laid now! I feel so silly, and so wet between my thighs! Can't we do it some more, Captain Gringo?"

"No. Captain Gringo has a schooner to catch. Big black schooner that leaves at midnight. You got that, Inez? Captain Gringo is leaving at midnight aboard a coastal schooner, if any of your other pals want to know."

She didn't answer. But her lips formed the words. That was probably good enough.

He checked her eyelid to make sure she hadn't overdone it. The lucky bitch was out like a light but would probably live. He dragged the dead cop over by the window for her, patted the uniform down, and robbed the corpse as any alley thug would be expected to. Anything he and Gaston couldn't use would go into the harbor easily enough when they got back to the yacht. The guy's gun wasn't bad. But that would be the first thing to get rid of, of course.

He locked the dead policeman and the sleeping police informant in together and went downstairs. The taproom was closed, but since the posada also served as an inn, the front door, while closed, wasn't locked.

Captain Gringo sat at the same table with the same Madeira bottle, now empty and hence unsuspicious, and it only took another million years before Gaston showed up looking like he'd been dragged through the keyhole, backward. The little

Frenchman sat down at the same table and gasped, "Sacre God damn, it's *hot* out there! Is there anything left in that bottle?"

"No. You wouldn't have liked it, anyway. Are the shops opening up again outside?"

"Some of them. The owners must really be ambitious. We know La Siesta is officially over. They know La Siesta is officially over, but the *sun* out there . . . merde alors!"

Captain Gringo said, "Can't be helped. I need a new hat. I mean right now. Better pick up another jacket while I'm at it. This outfit's been made by a police informer, and she may wake up before we can get those greenhorns out of town. Let's go. I'll tell you about it along the way."

Gaston called him an animal, too. But as they followed what shade there was back to the main drag, Gaston said he'd recruited almost thirty porters in the poorer favelas of an already poor town, and that they'd all been told to report to the yacht before sundown. Captain Gringo didn't ask how many unpaid women would be tagging along. There were always too many.

They found a men's shop open for business. Captain Gringo used some of the dead cop's last pay to buy a straw sombrero and a tan bolero jacket not much warmer to wear than the linen jacket he had on—and that Inez would remember.

He changed in an alley a block from the shop. Then, feeling better, he led Gaston to an open-air cantina, not the one Inez had worked at, and bought them tall, cool drinks with some of the change that cop had been carrying. As they relaxed, he filled Gaston in on his run-in with the law. Gaston found most of it amusing, but said, "I would have killed the woman too."

Captain Gringo shrugged and said, "Call me a sentimental cuss, or call me smart. Two bodies would have been harder to dispose of, and this way old Inez has to help, to save her own wicked ass!"

"Unless she just runs screaming to the police, wicked ass and all."

"Thought of that too. That's why I told her I'd still be in town well after dark. Nobody should be looking for us in all this heat *before* then."

The natives Gaston had recruited hither and yon started showing up at the yacht in dribs and drabs around sundown, and Gaston started putting them to work or firing them, depending on whether they wanted to work. The expedition members were completely confused by the semi-controlled chaos. Captain Gringo, Gaston, and Hardiman's crew were used to Hispanic work habits and were thus only mildly confused.

Professor Slade was a born clock-watcher, even by American standards. So after he'd gotten in the way a few times, Captain Gringo dragged him back to the poop where his wife and the other women were sitting, sat him down by old Elvira, and told them both, "If you ever expect to get this show on the road, leave the details to us guys who at least speak Spanish. When you wave your arms and yell at a native peon in English, he doesn't work faster. He just stops what he's doing and waits politely for you to say something he understands, see?"

Slade protested, "Half of them aren't doing *anything* whether one yells at them or not. I'm not paying people to just stand around and grin like idiots."

He pointed ashore and added, "Look at that one, for God's sake! He's sitting on a supply box strumming a guitar! Do you call that working, Dick?"

Captain Gringo shook his head and said, "No, I call it resting. That particular guy just helped us manhandle a piano-size crate down a narrow gangplank, and you can see he doesn't weigh a hundred and twenty. We're going to have to break open some of those packing cases and parcel your supplies out in lighter loads, by the way. We've sent a couple of guys into town to get us some tarps and rope."

Miss O'Connor pointed and chimed in, "Oh look, two of

the native girls are dancing to that young man's guitar now. Is that the Mexican hat dance, Dick?''

He said, "No. This isn't Mexico and they don't have a hat to dance on.'' Slade groaned. So he added, "We're not paying the mujeres the porters are bringing along,'' and Slade snapped, "We'll still have to *feed* them, damn it! I don't see why they want to bring their women along in the first place!''

His wife blushed and said, "Oh Huggy Bear, don't be so dense!'' as the redhead just blushed and didn't say anything. It was too stupid a question to answer. So Captain Gringo told her to keep her huggy bear out of the way and went back ashore.

He saw Hardiman talking to a couple of guys in white uniforms. Uniforms made him nervous. But he went over to see what was going on, anyway.

They were customs inspectors. They kept saying they had to examine all the bales and boxes Hardiman was landing on their fair shores, and Hardiman kept telling them it would be over his dead body. One of the customs inspectors was starting to look sleepy as he murmured politely about how easily that could be arranged. Captain Gringo saw that, for an old tropic hand, Hardiman had a lot to learn about arguing with a guy who had to be almost full-blooded Indian. So he nudged the skipper and said, "Gaston needs your help with the bill of lading. I'll handle this.''

Hardiman growled, "There's nothing to handle, damn it! The professor has a license from the central government. These jerk-offs have no authority to paw through his supplies, and even if they did, I'm not about to let them break open all this shit. I want to get it all ashore before the next ebb tide so I can get the fuck out of here!''

Captain Gringo took him by the arm, crunched down hard, and growled back in English pig Latin, "Amscray, odddammit-gay. You're getting us into an ightfay, you erkjay!''

Hardiman wandered off, muttering under his breath about not being afraid of any goddam greasers born of mortal woman. But at least he wandered off.

Captain Gringo smiled at the customs inspector with the Apache fuses smoldering in his opaque, inky eyes and said,

"You'll have to forgive him. He means well, but he doesn't understand our ways."

The Indio looked as if he were having a hell of a time staying awake as he murmured softly, "*Our* ways, Señor? I mean no disrespect, but you look like a fucking gringo to me."

The soldier of fortune laughed easily and said, "I used to be a fucking gringo, until I lost a few fights. That's why I want to avoid this one."

"Oh, are you afraid of me, Señor?"

"Of course. Only an idiot is not afraid to fight a man he's never seen fight. You could be tougher than me. I could be tougher than you. But since we are both men of reason, with nothing to fight about, let's not. What seems to be the trouble here?"

The more civilized of the two let out a sigh of relief and said, "El Señor is most simpatico. The problem is not difficult to men of reason. As you see, we are customs inspectors. Our job is to inspect goods being imported into Honduras. That red-faced friend of yours said we have no authority to do so. I assure you we do."

Captain Gringo nodded and said, "Of course you do. You can see Captain Hardiman's not too bright. Shall I send for our bill of lading? The trade winds have been dead all day and it may save you some hot, dusty work."

The sullen-looking one, who now looked only sullen instead of pissed-Apache, said, "Your Hardiman showed us his papers. We agreed they seemed in order. We agreed your professor had a valid license from the central government for to unload his expedition supplies duty-free. It was when we said we had to make sure you were unloading just what the papers said you should be unloading that the fool began to question our authority."

Captain Gringo nodded knowingly, looked around as if to make sure he wouldn't be overheard, and confided, "He's sweet on a muchacha here in Puerto Nogales. An expensive one. She expects, ah, gifts from her Yanqui sailor boy, if you get what I mean."

The one who'd seemed the more stubborn of the pair

laughed in a surprisingly boyish way and said, "I *knew* he was hiding something! Did the asshole really think we'd make a fuss about a little French perfume or a dozen silk stockings?"

Captain Gringo laughed too, and said, "Well, he is an asshole, and, man to man, I think he may have some American whiskey hidden somewhere in one crate or another."

He took out his wallet as he added, "Look, it's not worth getting him all excited again. What would the duty be on, say, a gross of silk stockings and a case of whiskey? I'm sure he isn't trying to smuggle that much in. But let's not argue about it."

They both stared soberly as he fingered the bills in his wallet thoughtfully. The now much friendlier Indio said, "Fifty lempiras should do it. You understand, of course, we still have to at least go through the motions, Señor?"

"Of course. God forbid anyone should think this was a *bribe*! Let me see . . . there's a case that's already open."

He led them to the nearest packing crate a few yards away as they split the bills he'd handed them and pocketed them. He'd carried the crate off himself. So he knew it was too light to have weapons or ammo in it. He unfastened the lid and opened the crate like a big cigar box. It was filled with sheets and mosquito netting. The more Indian-looking customs inspector hunkered down to paw through the contents, making an elaborate show of running one hand under the whole mess. It cost him a splinter in a knuckle. He cursed and stood up, sucking his injured paw. Then he said, "You are right, this is hot, dusty work when the trades are not blowing, Señor. We have your word you know of no other petty smuggling?"

Captain Gringo nodded, but said, "I can't swear none of the others have expensive girl friends here. But it hardly seems likely, since we're pushing inland as soon as we finish unloading."

It worked. They agreed with his considered opinion and wandered off to drink some of the "duty" they meant to turn in to their government the day hell froze over. Hardiman almost blew it by rushing up to Captain Gringo while they were still almost within earshot and hissing, "You crazy bastard! Why did you let them open that crate just now? Have you forgotten the guns and ammo that's not on the official bill of lading?''

Captain Gringo snorted in disgust and said, ''You sure talk dumb, for a professional gunrunner. They had to look at *something*. They had to make something on the deal. You owe me a hundred bucks, U.S., by the way. The going bribe here is fifty lempiras.''

''Bullshit! I didn't offer those greasers anything. You did, you chump! I told you me and Breslin had things fixed here. It wouldn't have cost us anything if we'd just stood our ground like men!''

''Maybe. Then again, maybe not. When a Latin argues, yelling, he's just arguing. When they go sleepy and quiet on you, they're usually not kidding. Your partner Breslin is not to be found these days, and those guys were acting ignorant as hell about a fix. Has it occurred to you that one guy covered with tar and feathers looks a lot like any other guy covered with tar and feathers, after he's dead?''

Hardiman blanched, but said, ''Bullshit. Old Breslin's seen his revolutions come and go. If he ain't in town, he's out at one of his trading posts in the jungle. You've got that map I gave you where it won't get lost?''

''Sure. The professor's map is mostly blank paper with an X where he expects to find his lost city. It won't be too far out of the way if we sort of stop for the night at Breslin's Numero Dos on the Rio Verde. I know this is none of my business, but I couldn't help noticing you still have numero cases of .30-30 still on board.''

''You let me worry about them, Walker. There's no way in hell even the nutty old professor would let you drag that much bang-bang along without asking questions. You just get that machine gun, those rifles, and the ammo I gave you to go with 'em to Breslin's jungle post, and your part of the deal is done.''

Captain Gringo shook his head wearily and said, ''Some deal. So far, aside from not getting paid, I'm out a hundred of my own money. Money I took off another guy, that is. From here on, anything coming out of my pocket will be *mine*, and I'm starting to feel pretty Apache already."

He turned away and walked through the confusion of crates and slow-moving natives to where Gaston was seated on a pile of supplies, smoking a perfecto and staring pensively out to sea. Captain Gringo said, "Well, we have all their shit ashore, and as soon as those guys get back with the stuff to bundle it more sensibly, we can move it out."

Gaston pointed the cigar at the purple horizon and said, "Observe that steamship plume glowing golden in the gloaming out there, Dick. It looks as if another banana boat is standing off the bar waiting for the tide to shift, hein?"

"Yeah, they sure load lots of bananas around here. So what?"

"So why don't we just wait and see if its next port of call is to the south instead of to the north? I find hiking through jungles très fatigué."

"I've noticed. In the first place, if that is a banana boat it's sure to head right back to the States while said bananas are still green. If it's not a banana boat, it may be a gunboat, and I find them très fatigué, too. In the second place, I thought we agreed this expedition is the best cover to be found around here right now. Oh yeah, in the third, a dame's about to wake up any minute with a cop I had to kill, and I'd sure like to be somewhere else when that happens. If she remembers what I told her to remember, they'll be *expecting* us to be somewhere along this waterfront later tonight. So let's not *be* here, okay?"

Gaston said, "I follow you, to a point. Where even you can lead us from here, by land, is more difficult to grasp. Nobody who has not been down here as long as me seems able to grasp that these Central American countries are only tiny on the *map*! People get lost in the jungles of Panama, and all the jungles of Panama could get lost in the one you seem hell-bent on dragging me into!"

"Look, did we get lost in the Amazon jungle that time?"

"As a matter of fact, we did. We'd *still* be lost in it if we had not made friends with those oversexed native girls! I've been talking to these peones about the natives in the jungles nearer at hand. They tell me the natives are not oversexed. They are simply très savage and—this will cheer you—given to putting six-foot reed arrows into people. *Poisoned* six-foot arrows.''

''Did they say what tribe we're liable to have the most trouble with?''

''Oui, *all* of them. One gathers the local warlord, Don Nogales, does not get along with Indians, either. None of these pobrecitos from town speaks any of their wilder cousins' dialects. I gather they are most afraid of the Sambo bands. You know about the Sambo, of course?''

''As in 'Little Black Sambo?' ''

''Not exactly. Sambo may be an African word, but here it does not refer to an amusing child who plays with tigers. The Sambo, like the Black Caribs, are a truculent mixture of already truculent Indians and runaway slaves.''

''Ouch. What about the local Mosquitos?''

''They are called Mosquitos here for the same reason they are called Mosquitos all along the Mosquito Coast. They *sting*! The Sambo are said to charge with màchetes and an inborn dislike for white people. Our peones mentioned Pipil and Chorti, too. Different languages and customs; the same unpleasant attitude to strangers in their neck of the bushes. Has it yet occurred to you that the nearest civilization, once we leave here, is a très formidable march, even if the trail was not tossed salad infested by snakes, savages, and other wild animals?''

''Sure, and has it ever occurred to you that if it's one thing Puerto Nogales is, civilized it ain't? Let's get this show on the road. I'd rather explain that dead cop to wild Indians than guys who just found out about tar and feathers and think it's fun!''

The sun was down long before the expedition moved out. But the moon was up, and in the tropics, a full moon beat a noonday sun for illumination on the dusty trail. The first few hours were spent slogging along a baked-mud wagon trace with banana plantations on either side. It was monotonous but fortunate that the first leg of the journey was wide, firm, and flat. Even so, they were moving slow as hell.

The porters, though carrying all the crap, could have pushed on faster. An excited snail could have pushed on faster. The four white women with the party had changed into reasonably sensible outfits consisting of mosquito boots, whipcord riding habits, and veiled, broad-brimmed hats of straw or, in Elvira Slade's case, canvas-covered pith like her husband's. The professor and his seven male assistants looked like white hunters on safari in Darkest Africa. Any one of the barefoot peon girls scampering along with the porters could have run rings around them.

Captain Gringo had noticed right off that everyone as white as he and Gaston were wearing spanking-new boots. A couple of the guys were starting to limp already. So he didn't call a trail break the next time one was due. He knew that once feet started to blister, it hurt worse to start up again than to just keep walking, and he knew Don Nogales would probably frown on their making their first night fires among his banana stalks.

A couple of Slade's men were carrying rifles as they scouted the cultivated land on either side for wild beasts about to charge. Captain Gringo made a mental note that they were even greener than the girls. One was called Wayne and the other was Baldwin. He knew two of the girls were supposed to be actresses. Wayne and Baldwin were taking their roles pretty seriously, too. He wondered what the hell actors and actresses were doing on a scientific expedition. Maybe nobody else knew much about the Edison cameras that took motion pictures. He'd read, just before leaving the States, that someone had started a motion-picture studio in New Jersey and that people were actually willing to pay a penny to watch other people flirt or throw pies at each other as one cranked the handle of the penny machine. Some people would pay to see anything.

Gaston fell in beside him to say, "I just moved up and down the line. Some of our porters are making their mujeres help with the packs, and when a macho mestizo lets a mere woman know he's getting tired, take it from me, he's about to drop!''

Captain Gringo said, ''I know. The others are tripping over rocks that aren't there, too. See if anybody knows how far we are from the tree line, or at least a fallow field.''

Gaston dropped back to talk to the locals. One of the professor's guys, called Blake, took Gaston's place at Captain Gringo's side and panted, ''We're going to have to stop, damn it. The girls are tired.''

Captain Gringo kept moving at the same slow but mile-eating pace as he replied, ''I haven't heard any screams of maidenly distress, Blake. Next time you buy new boots, break 'em in before you do any serious walking.''

''Oh, *I'm* not tired. I'm just concerned about the others.''

''Don't be. It's Professor Slade's expedition and I'm in charge of moving it. We've still got some moonlight to go and some miles to travel. What's your job, aside from bitching, I mean?''

''I'm one of the writers. I write plays and filmscripts.''

''That sounds like honest employment, at least. But how come Slade needs a scriptwriter along on a scientific expedition, for Pete's sake?''

''To write the narration, of course. We're going to make a full film record of our expedition, and, naturally, people who come to the theater to see it will expect us to say something about the pictures they're looking at.''

''That sounds reasonable. How do you get to talk, on film? Gramophone records or something?''

''No, they tried that and it didn't work so well. Edison can't get the phonograph synchronized with the projector. Each scene will have a written explanation flashed on the screen between shots, see?''

Captain Gringo tried to picture it and grinned. He was too polite to say, ''Right. Here you are about to see us walking a lot through the rain forest and, coming up, you'll see us walking the other way through the rain forest.'' He supposed if they actually found anything but trees where the professor's map said a white goddess had built a three-sided pyramid,

Blake might come in handy. He didn't seem good for anything else.

Blake proved he was right by insisting, "I mean it, Travis. This is far enough. I insist you stop to let the women rest."

The taller American said flatly, "You're not in a position to insist on anything, Blake. I take my orders from the guy who pays me, and if he gives me too many I'm liable to quit. Why don't you take your boots off and try walking barefoot? This wagon trace is solid 'dobe, no worse than the sidewalks you're obviously more used to."

"Don't get snotty with me, Travis. I can't abide hired help who doesn't know its own place!"

"Don't worry about my place, Sonny. I don't work for you. And your place will be flat on your ass if you don't watch that mouth. Why is it a sissy always seems to be the one who wants to give orders?"

"Who are you calling a sissy, you unwashed beachcomber?"

Captain Gringo sighed and said, "Okay, we can probably find enough room over in those bananas for a private fistfight, unless you'd rather have a regular duel."

Blake blanched and gasped. "Don't be absurd. I'm an author, not a prizefighter! Whatever gave you the idea I was looking for a fistfight with anyone?"

"Just a general impression, I guess. Go bother someone else, Blake. Guys like you bore the shit out of me."

Blake must have been able to take a hint. He dropped back to bitch about him to Professor Slade. They were too far back for Captain Gringo to hear Slade's answers as Blake's louder whines followed him like the annoying hum of a mosquito trying to find a hole in the netting around a four-poster late at night.

He heard lighter boot heels overtaking him as he just kept walking. Miss O'Connor fell in beside him, saying, "Some of the others are starting to complain about this pace you're setting, Dick."

He said, "I know. So far, you're the prettiest, Miss . . . ?"

She said her first name was Meabh, pronouncing it "mauve." He asked her if her feet were hurting too, and she said, "Only a little. Your friend Gaston just told me we'd stop for the night as soon as you find a place we can build some fires. Does he ever tell white lies?''

He chuckled and said, ''I do. Once I let any of you take the boots off your blisters, we figure to be stuck awhile. You don't really want to spend all day tomorrow in a banana grove, do you?''

She said, ''I don't know. I've never been in a banana grove at all. What's wrong with camping under banana trees, Dick?''

''Lousy shade and lots of bugs. Big ones. All sorts of creepy-crawlies like bananas as much as we do, and all sorts of even bigger bugs like to eat *them*. It might be fun to see the expression on old Blake's face the first time a spider as big as his hand crawls across it. But you girls deserve a nicer campsite. Aside from fist-size spiders, and snakes who hunt fist-size spiders in banana groves, there's not enough room between the stalks to pitch any tents, and if you think sitting under bananas when the sun is shining is grim, wait until you try it under a tropic rain!''

''You've convinced me!'' The redhead laughed, adding, ''I told them you had to know more about conditions down here than any of us. How long have you been down here, Dick?''

''Too long,'' he said, not wanting to go into it. Aside from the fact he was supposed to be some guy named Travis right now, the true story of the misadventures that had made him a renegade soldier of fortune were more depressing than interesting, even to him.

To change the subject, he asked her what she did for Professor Slade; and Meabh said, ''I'm a mythologist.''

He frowned thoughtfully as he tried to figure out what she meant. She must have been used to that. For she went on, ''I collect and record the myths of various cultures. It all started when I wrote a term paper about the Anglo-Saxon mythology about Celtic mythology. You've no idea how silly English fairy tales based on Celtic folk tales can get unless you have the Gaelic.''

''I thought you just might be Irish, Meabh. Do you really speak Gaelic? I thought that was against the law these days.''

She sighed and said, ''Glory be to the potato famine, my

people left the Four Green Fields before they could hang everyone for the wearing of the green. I was brought up in Brooklyn, where it's not as dangerous to be Irish. I have the Gaelic; French, of course; and I'm working on my Spanish. You see, if you don't know just what people *mean* when you take down their mythology, you can wind up with a dreadfully silly account; and worse yet, people reading what you've written in English have no way of tripping you up. Did you know, for instance, there was no such thing as a Druid?''

He laughed and said, ''Not now, for sure. The Druids were the priests of the Irish old-time religion, right?''

''Wrong. It all began with that Italian Caesar not understanding half of what the poor Gauls were trying to explain or, in the case of their private mysteries, trying to get out of telling him. It's all so simple as soon as you know that the word 'druith,' or 'druid,' means 'secret,' even in modern Scots Gaelic.''

He laughed and said, ''Simple for you, maybe. I thought you just said there *were* no druids.''

''There were secrets they didn't tell outsiders. *Those* were druids. As to what the secrets were, or who knew them, I'm still working on that. The so-called Druid religion had been stamped out, even before the coming of the Saxon. So most of it died with the old Ollies who went to their graves with their druids never written down, see?''

''Oh God, what's an Ollie?''

''A wise man, a scholar, perhaps it could translate as 'priest.' ''

''Oh, then the real Druids were the Ollies who called secrets 'druids'?''

''We think they may have been. As I said, so much nonsense has been written about the pagan beliefs of the Celts. But let's talk about the *Indian* beliefs I've come to record. Do you have any Maya or Aztec to teach me, Dick?''

He shook his head and said, ''Not classic Aztec or Maya. The Spanish didn't approve of the wearing of the green, either, and . . . that's funny.''

''What's funny, Dick?''

''Green was the sacred color of both cultures, and I don't

think they were as closely related as most people think. Even though they're mostly wearing pants these days, some tribes still speak dialects of both old languages. Thanks to some book-burning, not even they can read the old glyphs, of course. The local Mosquito and Pipil tribes speak a lingo at least related to Aztec. I know, because Comanche is, too, and some Comanche I picked up in Texas one time almost works on Mosquitos. The Honduran Chorti are supposed to sort of understand Quiche, which is as close to ancient Maya as anyone gets today.''

''Oh, do you know any Maya, Dick?''

''Just a few words. Learned *that* in Mexico one time. 'Bei' means yes and 'ma' means no. End of the lesson, for now. I see real trees ahead at last. Thank God. Even *my* legs are starting to go. I may have been getting too much exercise lately.''

She asked, ''Will you teach me some more after we make camp for the night, Dick?''

He said he would, not sure just what she had in mind but sincerely hoping it wasn't Quiche-Maya sentence structure. He wasn't sure he wanted to parse Quiche-Maya even if he knew how. But he might be up to some basic biology once he got his boots off and some coffee and grub in his gut. He hadn't had a woman for at least eight hours.

Setting up camp went more smoothly than expected, since the moon was still up and most of the greenhorns stayed flat where they'd fallen as soon as he told them they didn't have to trudge any farther on their blistered feet. Gaston had been keeping an eye out for talent as they'd led the porters and their mujeres this far from the seaport. So he only had to show a few picked men how to pitch the first tent and they did the rest.

The professor had brought along eight tents. More than enough for the whites in the party. Tough shit about the natives if it rained. But the Hondurans were good mâchete men, and some got to work building lean-to shelters before the last canvas tents were up. All shelter was, of course, built ring-around-the-main-fire, Indian style, with smaller individual fires before each tent to dry socks and bare feet, and to discourage the bugs from flapping about the smaller lamps lit in some of the tents. A palm-size moth could drive you nuts trying to fly inside an oil lamp. But once any bug flew into an open flame, it was through for the evening.

Captain Gringo and Gaston had been issued a tent of their own to share, and better yet, had agreed to take turns standing watch until they figured out if any of the other men in the party were any good at all. Professor Slade had asked why they had to stand guard at all, this close to town. So there went Slade as a possible night-watch commander.

Nobody else seemed to want to bother Captain Gringo as he sat cross-legged on the ground in front of his tent, full of coffee and Boston beans. He was glad he and Gaston wouldn't be inside the stuffy tent at the same time tonight. Frijoles didn't make one fart much, but Boston beans were not what he'd have fed tired people in the tropics.

The coffee was good, though. It was the first New Orleans chicory brew he'd had in some time, and while the local coffee was as good as coffee got, it made for a piquant change.

He didn't want to do anything but sit there sipping coffee and smoking good tobacco for the next few years or so. So he cursed pretty good when he heard a fight breaking out on the far side of the main fire and got wearily to his feet to knock heads together.

As he circled the fire, he saw the American author, Blake, standing over a peon on the ground as the other cotton-clad natives watched in sober silence all around. As Captain Gringo came closer, Blake pointed at the much smaller Honduran he'd decked and spat, "I ordered this idiot to carry my luggage to my tent and he just grinned at me."

"Naturally you told him what you wanted in Spanish?"

Before Blake could answer, the peon youth rolled to his hands and knees to rise, which seemed reasonable. But then Captain Gringo spotted the gleam of firelight on cold steel and kicked him flat again before he could put that knife in his hand anywhere important.

Then, since he was a fair-minded man, Captain Gringo hauled off and sucker-punched Blake flush on the jaw, knocking him out as well as ass over teakettle. The crowd of porters and their mujeres gasped collectively but not unappreciatively. One of the native girls giggled and observed, "He seems most justo as well as muy toro, no?"

That had been the general idea. The peon he'd kicked was still semiconscious. So Captain Gringo told him, "Put that blade away. If you ever flash it around me again, I'll kill you."

The youth sat up, stared soberly at the unconscious Blake nearby, and asked, "May I flash it at *that* mother-fucker, Señor?"

Captain Gringo smiled thinly and replied, "No. If I'd wanted him stabbed, I'd have let you stab him."

"Si, but he *hit* me, por nada! What if he hits me again, Señor?"

"I don't think he will."

An older man in the rapidly growing crowd stepped forward, saying, "Es verdad. It is over, Hernan. Let me help you to your feet, with El Señor's permission, of course."

Captain Gringo nodded, and the older guy hauled the kid up and out of reach, saying sensible, soothing things to him as he led him away into the darkness. By this time almost everyone in camp, including the whites, had come to see the show. The brown-haired girl Captain Gringo thought might be Miss Burnes dropped to her knees by the unconscious Blake and cradled his head in the lap of her tan whipcords as she gasped, "Oh Lord, is poor Bruce hurt badly? What happened to him?"

Captain Gringo said, "I hit him. He's not hurt half as bad as he'll be if he ever pulls such a dumb stunt again."

Miss Burnes stared up at him as if he'd just sprouted horns and a tail. Professor Slade said, "I demand an explanation for this unseemly behavior, Travis!"

So Captain Gringo said, "I didn't behave unseemly. He did, and since we're speaking English, I may as well tell you

I saved his life. The jerk-off ordered a native in English and then hit him when he wasn't understood. That's not how you get these people to obey you, Prof. It's how you get yourself and maybe others killed when you're outnumbered pretty good by simple people with a simple idea of justice. Their first commandment goes something like, You hurt me and if I can't hurt you my friends and relations are sure gonna try!''

Slade sighed and said, "Oh God, we've barely gotten started and we've already got a mutiny on our hands?"

Captain Gringo shook his head, but called out in Spanish, "El patron wishes to know if it is over. May I tell him it is over, Muchachas y Muchachos?"

He was answered with a round of happy voices, and a clearer voice called out, "In God's truth, we know a fair-minded patron when we get the chance for to work for one!"

Another man added wistfully, "Si, it does not happen very often."

Captain Gringo turned back to Slade and said, "I think they're still on our side for now. I'll get Blake to his tent and take the first watch."

Slade nodded, but asked, "What are you watching out for, if you don't expect more trouble, Dick?"

Captain Gringo said, "I said I didn't expect any more trouble tonight, here in camp. The woods haven't been heard from yet. That's why somebody has to be out there circling with a gun while the rest of you catch some sleep, see?"

"But, Dick, we're only a few miles from Puerto Nogales! Are we talking about Indians or bandits?"

Captain Gringo shrugged and said, "I don't know who might be out there in the dark. That's why I'm taking along a Krag as well as my thirty-eight."

He could see he was upsetting his greenhorns. So he added, "I don't really expect anyone to try anything this close to Don Nogales' bananas. Don Nogales wouldn't like it. But it's better to be safe than sorry."

Meabh O'Connor asked, "Have you ever run into trouble this close to town, Dick?"

He knew by now old Inez would be awake again and doing whatever came most naturally to her. But he didn't think they wanted to hear about the cop he'd had to kill that afternoon right in the middle of town. So he just smiled and said, "It happens."

The moon was down. It didn't matter. It would have been black as a bitch under the thick forest canopy, anyway, as Captain Gringo circled slowly and silently counter-clockwise, far enough out to have anyone within pistol shot of the camp outlined against the glow of its night fires and tent lamps. He wasn't really expecting to, this early in the game. So he carried his borrowed Krag slung from his right shoulder.

But since he wouldn't have been pulling night picket in the first place if he hadn't thought trouble was at least possible, he couldn't smoke. The idea was to spot possible trouble before it spotted him.

Had it been up to him, he wouldn't have been packing a military Krag, either. The Scandinavian bolt-action repeater was the current fashion in military circles. It was a good battlefield weapon with a killing range of almost a mile in the hands of a good shot. But for close-in brush popping, he'd have favored the older Winchester .44-40 or, better yet, a 12-gauge Browning pump. They both threw more, faster, at the ranges one figured to have to in heavy jungle. If they ran into trouble from either Indians or ladrones, the fight could be decided one way or the other in the time it took to crank any bolt-action rifle dry.

He understood trouble with ladrones. A thief was a thief any time or place. The talk about Indian trouble had him a bit bemused. Most Central American tribes, no matter what their reputation, seemed to just want strangers to leave them the hell alone. The Spanish Conquest had settled the hash of those few local primitives devoted to warfare as a blood sport. Those still clinging to their old ways tended to be defensive survivalists who only fought when they had to.

Some of them had to, a lot, because their Spanish-speaking Christian cousins tended to exploit them. More than one

Hispanic Lothario had had his ardor for a naked Mosquito Minnihaha cooled considerably by a six-foot reed arrow replacing his original six-inch erection. But Captain Gringo and Gaston had so far managed to get along with both male and female Mosquitos simply by treating them as human beings. Chorti and Pipil had to have similar live-and-let-live notions if they shared the same woods with the deadly-when-annoyed Mosquitos. The Sambo sounded like Black Caribs, and in his time, he and Gaston had even managed to avoid a fight with Black Caribs, albeit not so easily. If the local tribes were up in arms, there could only be one answer: someone had been messing with them.

Captain Gringo didn't intend to mess with Indians. So he put idle worries about them aside for now and kept an eye on the tricky light from the camp as it shifted according to where he was at the moment. The tents and lean-to's blocked the campfire glow into dull orange shafts across the forest floor, of course. But some of the tents themselves looked sort of like big square Japanese lanterns glowing weirdly because of the oil lamps inside them. He knew that his greenhorns, in spite of their fatigue, were still too keyed up by their new, and to them exotic, surroundings to sleep, even though it was past midnight now. Off to his right a jaguar screamed from the depths of the dark jungle. He chuckled, muttering, "If that didn't wake 'em up, nothing will."

As an old jungle hand, he was reassured rather than alarmed by the ghastly noise. Jaguars only yelled like that when they wanted to get laid. If anything on two legs had been anywhere within a country mile of that big cat just now, it would have kept quiet as a mouse.

As he circled farther, he heard another noise he couldn't figure. He frowned, unslung the Krag, and homed in on it as he tried to decide what it was and where it was coming from. It sounded something like a big rusty sewing machine. It was coming from one of the tents down the curved line of the camp, which worried him less than if it had been coming from the jungle *around* the camp, but it still confused him.

The tent was not only illuminated from inside, its light was flickering. And then, as he got a better view of its broad canvas end, he blinked and muttered, "What the hell?"

It was impossible. But it looked as if the end of the tent were made of glass, giving him a clear view of a naked white lady about eight feet tall taking it dog-style from a Chinaman even bigger. Then the penny dropped and he laughed softly. Someone was projecting a pornographic film on the wall of the tent from inside. Captain Gringo had only seen a couple of moving-picture shows in his life, none of them quite this dirty, and he hadn't known one could view the flickering images almost as well from the far side of the screen. He wondered what any Indian scouts creeping up on the camp would make of what looked pretty odd to him. Like most men of his generation, Captain Gringo had been raised to view a photograph as a small stationary picture in a frame. Edison and Eastman had only worked out moving pictures within the past five years or so. They took some getting used to.

The white lady, who looked French, or what every Victorian expected a French lady to look, turned over, grinning right at Captain Gringo and winking lewdly, as if she saw him there watching her. The Chinese gentleman dropped most of himself right out of the picture, as if into a pit under the tent, and proceeded to eat her for dessert. Captain Gringo couldn't help feeling a little awkward, even though his common sense told him she'd really been making those faces at the camera in some studio far away and long ago. Despite the flicker and lack of natural color, it still made him feel like a Peeping Tom and, worse yet, made him *want* some of that. She was really quite attractive, and if she didn't enjoy sex an awful lot, she was certainly a great actress.

But sex one couldn't have was not Captain Gringo's idea of a spectator sport, and aside from feeling silly standing there frustrated, he knew he was outlined by the light to anyone deeper in the jungle. So he moved on. He was out here to keep his greenhorns safe, not to pass judgment on their ideas of entertainment. As he turned his back on the Chinaman, just as he was starting to do it right to the French actress again, he wondered vaguely who was showing the stag film to whom. It was hard to keep the tents lined up in his head, from this side.

He knew, of course, that Slade had brought along a projector for viewing his hopefully more sedate shots of the expedition as they were developed by . . . yeah, it was probably old Simpson and Ferris trying out the projector. They were the lab technicians Slade had brought along, and they were sharing the same tent, along with their darkroom stuff and the projector. They'd obviously brought along some film that had already been developed. It was an interesting but sort of weird hobby. Captain Gringo doubted there was any way to make money off dirty moving pictures. How could one ever show them to the general public without causing a riot and getting arrested?

He passed a couple of native lean-to's without seeing or hearing anything. The natives, sensibly, had long since torn off a good-night piece and gone to sleep. He'd been out here for hours, damn it.

He passed another tent well illuminated from inside despite the hour. There was something projected on *its* canvas wall, too. But as he swung in closer to check it out, he saw it was the moving shadows of the people inside. They sure were moving a lot for this late at night. He shrugged and started to move on. Then he stopped and grinned as the shadow of a long, shapely limb rose like a cobra from its basket to wave a high heel back and forth, close to the canvas, and, yeah, if that wasn't the rounded rump of somebody humping hot and heavy, it had to be a big bald giant eating supper at the base of that waving leg. He couldn't help wondering where the other one was. Was she doing the split or something as the guy laid her good?

He knew it was none of his business. But on the other hand, there were only four women attached to the expedition. Three, when one considered old Elvira was taken for sure. So a guy might avoid needless embarrassment if he could find out who else was already spoken for in the nights to come.

She looked like she was coming indeed, now, as the other leg joined the first to wave at the tent roof against the glow of the oil lamp. He wondered why they'd left the lamp lit. Then he wondered why he'd wonder such a dumb thing. If the rest of her was shaped half as good as those two wild legs, *he'd* want to watch where he was going, too.

He moved cautiously closer on the balls of his feet—as if the lovers on the far side of the thin canvas would have noticed, had he been a steam locomotive bearing down on them. As he got close enough to hear, he heard her moaning, "Oh, faster, faster, faster, Huggy Bear!"

Captain Gringo managed not to laugh out loud. It wasn't easy. He'd suspected there was more to old Elvira than met the eye. She'd obviously been a stunner in her day and still wasn't bad. But he hadn't known the old professor could move his tail like that. He'd been walking sort of weary on the trail. But maybe if a guy lucked on to a wife like Elvira, he'd have started walking weary on his honeymoon. Captain Gringo walked on, smiling wistfully. It was nice to know the old couple still had the magic going for them.

A nut, a twig, or bat shit dropped off to his right. He froze, gun muzzle trained that way, and held his breath until he was pretty sure that was all he'd heard. The trouble with jungles was that something was always going bump in the night in them, even when nothing was there.

He moved on, passing more lean-to's and three dark tents in a row. Then he saw the shaft of campfire light ahead winking as someone or something walked along it. It was a little early for Gaston to relieve him. So he called out, "Alto, quien es?"

Professor Slade's voice replied, "Is that you, Travis?" and when Captain Gringo replied it wasn't the bogeyman, Slade came over to him, fully dressed, to say, "I've been looking for my wife. She stepped out some time ago to, ah, you know, heed the call of nature. I wonder if by any chance you'd seen her?"

Captain Gringo said, "I hardly ever watch ladies taking a crap." Which was as close to the truth as he could get without an outright lie. He added, just as truthfully in a way, "She isn't out here in the trees, Professor."

Slade sounded worried as he said, "I wonder where the

devil she could be, then. I just heard some sort of animal roaring out here and—''

''That was just a jaguar, Sir,'' Captain Gringo cut in, adding: ''I heard it, too. It was at least a mile from here, and they don't yell when they attack.''

He didn't add that, man-eating or not, jaguars sprang silently and went for the throat. Somehow he didn't think the already worried professor wanted to hear that. Slade nodded absently and took a step the way Captain Gringo had just come, saying, ''Well, I'll just circle the camp once before I go back to our tent.''

Captain Gringo grabbed his elbow with his free hand and swung him around, saying, ''I've already covered things that way, Professor. Come on, I'll keep you company as we, ah, search around the far side.''

It worked, to a point. But Slade kept asking him to move a little faster as from time to time he called out his wife's name in the dark. Normally, Captain Gringo would have shut him up. It was a hell of a way to walk a sneaky night picket. But while enemies farther out in the dark were only a fifty-fifty worry, Slade had someone hanging horns on him for *sure*, in camp. If the poor guy yelled loud enough, his cheating wife might have time to get her cheating ass back to their tent in time.

One of the native porters stood up behind his lean-to to ask them, in a tired voice, if they needed help with something. Captain Gringo told him to go back to sleep and added in an aside to Slade, ''We don't want the whole bunch charging out to look for her. Might not be delicate, if a peon found her, ah, straining a squat.''

''I'm not sure I should let you talk about my wife that way, young man,'' warned Slade, adding: ''Besides, she's never had any, ah, medical problems like that!'' Then he pursed his lips and said, ''Hmmm, come to think of it, there have been similar incidents like this in the past. I recall on the vessel coming down here, how I awoke one night to find her gone and . . . But that time it was seasickness, she said, not constipation.''

''Yeah, well, some women are delicate about such problems, even with their husband. We could be embarrassing her, yelling into the woods like this. Why don't you just go back to your tent and wait for her? I'll go on and circle the camp again, and if she's not back by then, we'll know we really have to look for her, right?''

Slade agreed, and Captain Gringo dropped him off at the next gap between the tents. He didn't allow himself to sigh with relief until the older man was out of earshot. The tent where they were holding the dirty picture show was only a few tents ahead, again. When he got to it, they'd stopped the fun and games for the night. That meant, as he'd assumed, they weren't using Slade's equipment that way with his approval.

The tent they'd been holding the other fun and games in was just as dark when he got to it. He chuckled and walked on, pleased with himself for letting the professor yell his head off like that just now. A few tents down, the light was on in a tent that had been dark before, and he heard old Elvira scolding hell out of her husband for being so silly. She said, ''I was just about to come when I heard you waking up the dead, Huggy Bear. Honestly, can't a girl enjoy a moment's privacy?''

Captain Gringo moved on, grimacing with distaste. He'd gotten the double meaning she put into even her excuses, and he wasn't sure whether he was more disgusted with her or with her stupid husband. It was small wonder she screwed around so much on the side. Guys like Slade gave their women a license to betray them. Elvira was lucky as hell she'd never married a Spaniard. They worked cheating the other way around. The guy got to cheat. The woman wound up dead if she smiled back at a waiter. But Captain Gringo knew, as well as Elvira, that Slade would never catch her; or if he did, he'd probably just stand there and sob like a big baby.

Captain Gringo wondered who the other man was. He decided he didn't really want to know. It was none of his business; he sort of liked old Slade; and he'd already hit one of the guys in the party.

Things calmed down and got back to boring as hell as he

slowly circled the camp for what felt like forever. Then, about an hour after he'd started calling Gaston a slugabed son of a bitch, over and over again, the little Frenchman came out yawning and said, "Eh bien, it's your turn to jack off in the tent. Would you like to leave a morning call?"

"If you wake me before noon, I'll kill you. We'll shelter here and rest them up till their legs and the setting sun make for better traveling conditions."

"All day, Dick? It won't be too hot for hiking, now that we are under the forest canopy, hein?"

"It'll be cool enough. It won't be dark enough. I want us moving under cover of darkness the first few marches. I hate surprises, and something odd's going on in this part of Honduras."

"Merde alors, you just noticed? Are we talking about people trailing us or people lying in wait for us, my old and cautious?"

"Don't know. Maybe both. But if they can't see us, they can't do anything to us. I'm not expecting any hostile moves this close to town. But a lot of people know where we're heading, including people we may not even know about. By the way, did you just lay the professor's wife?"

"Mon Dieu, what a droll suggestion! Should I have?"

"No, and you'd better not. I have enough to worry about. But two sets of eyes are better than one. So keep an eye on her. She's cheating on the poor old goat almost openly, and that could lead to problems we don't need."

"Oui, we have problems enough. May I make a practique suggestion, Dick?"

Captain Gringo shook his head and said, "I've already thought of just leading them toward the border and running for Guatemala. Aside from being a shitty trick, it's almost as dangerous as what we're doing now and not as profitable. Take over here. I've been on my feet enough tonight."

It was well after 3:00 A.M., but Captain Gringo had too much on his mind to sleep. Since they wouldn't be moving

out again for at least thirteen hours and it felt like rain, he
didn't even try. He sat cross-legged on his bedroll with the
two maps he'd been given to work with spread on the canvas
groundcloth of the tent in front of him, illuminated by the
hanging oil lamp overhead. Considering they were both maps
of the same area, drawn to about the same scale, they didn't
look much alike.

Professor Slade's map, printed in English, had a tight mesh
of latitudinal and longitudinal coordinates over mostly blank
paper, printed, "Jungle. Mostly Unexplored." Slade himself
had inked in the position of his lost Maya city, smack in the
middle of a lot of nothing that represented lots of trees,
swamps, and up and down, in the real world.

The map Hardiman had given him had been printed locally,
in Spanish, with fuzzier lines but more detail. Naturally there
was nothing on that map about lost cities. But the main
stream-drainage and, more important, jungle trails were there.
Some of them, in truth, were indicated by dotted lines with
question marks every few inches. But Captain Gringo found
where they were at the moment and, yeah, the wagon trace
they'd followed this far petered out to a gum-gatherer's trail
leading to another, leading at right angles to the trading post
where they were supposed to drop the extra weapons and
ammo off. Captain Gringo took out a pencil stub and lightly
traced a line from where they were to the trading post, then
dog-legged it onto the mysterious X. It didn't take them far
out of the way, and went nowhere near any of the trails any
sneak might have on his own map. Captain Gringo had
learned, the hard way, that while ambushes were usually set
up along trails, it was almost as easy to navigate through
really dense jungle *off* the trails as *on* them.

This seeming paradox was occasioned by the way vegetation
naturally grew in the tropics. In such a wet, warm climate the
only limitation an inspired vegetable had to worry about was
light. There were plants, half of them unknown to science,
that could grow in water, on soggy soil, on dry soil, and,
hell, on bare rock. But not in deep shade. So, once the
first-come-first-served trees got big enough to shade the forest
floor in cathedral gloom even at high noon, nothing much else

could sprout. It was along the *edges* of trails and rivers, where the sun could get at the warm, moist soil, that the classic green-hell jungle grew too thick to push through without a mâchete. In the tall timber, one could walk for miles without tripping over a dandelion. The trick was not to get lost.

One buttress-rooted forest giant looked an awful lot like the one right next to it, even when they were different species. So one had to navigate as if at sea, by compass and dead reckoning. In this case, that shouldn't be too tough, and a lot safer. Captain Gringo had two maps as well as a pocket compass. He meant to leave the known trails to others, friends or enemies. There was a lot of that going around, down here.

Something scratched at the tent flap like kitten claws, and he heard a familiar voice whisper, "Are you decent, Dick?"

Then, before he could answer, Meabh O'Connor ducked inside, adding, "Oh, there you are. I just thought of something. Could the name of the Maya Hero-God, Kukulkan, be spelled with 'c's' instead of 'k's'?"

He blinked in bewilderment as she plopped down on the bedroll beside him. Not because of her question, but because she was only wearing a terry-cloth robe and hadn't fastened the front too securely. He said, "You'd have to if you were spelling it in Spanish. There's no letter 'k' in the Spanish alphabet."

"Oh? What about the 'k' in 'Moskito Coast'?"

"English maps. I guess they're trying to keep from confusing the Mosquito Indians with the kind that buzz around outside mosquito netting. But there's still no 'k' in the Spanish alphabet, and 'mosquito' is a Spanish word. It means 'little fly.' Is there any point to this discussion, Meabh?"

She sounded a bit breathless as she answered, "Yes, it just occurred to me how close the Maya 'Cuculcan' is to the Gaelic 'Cuchulainn'! You know who *he* was, don't you?"

Captain Gringo laughed and said, "Sort of. Cuchulainn was something like the Sir Lancelot of Irish mythology. Ran around killing giants, dragons, and anyone else dumb enough to be anywhere near him of a Saturday night when he had his Irish up, right?''

She didn't laugh. She said, ''The timing is right. Maya civilization was contemporary with our Dark Ages. Maya myth would have it that around four to eight hundred A.D., a white wizard appeared from out of the sea with a band of companions and ruled as their teacher and king for only a few years before he sailed away to the east, promising to return if they ever needed him, remember?''

Captain Gringo said, ''I don't remember. But the legend got the Aztecs in an awful mess when Cortez showed up. They didn't have *their* lost boss wizard down as Kukulkan. They thought his name was Quetzalcoatl.''

''Oh pooh, that was simply the Aztec translation of the Maya 'Kukulkan.' Both mean 'feathered serpent' and the Maya saw him first.''

''If you say so. But don't you see that if the Maya's mysterious white whatever was called the feathered serpent, he . . . What the hell does the name 'Cuchulainn' mean?''

''The hound of cullan. It's my thesis the Maya changed a name that meant nothing to them to one that did, simply by changing a few letters. 'Cuculcan' is so *close* to 'Cuchulainn,' Dick! Can't you see that?''

He shrugged and said, ''Yeah, but I can't see a mess of ancient Irishmen arriving at least a thousand years before Columbus, can you?''

''Why not?'' she demanded, adding: ''How did you think the Celts got to the Emerald Island in the first place, on bikes? We didn't *always* dig spuds, you know. 'Murphy' means 'sailor,' and it's the most common name in Ireland. It's not true we only paddled about in little basketwork fishing boats. Caesar records sea battles with the Celts of Britain, and the Romans *lost* more than one of them. Our galleys were bigger, with oaken sides too stout for the Roman rams, and had great leather sails that could tack to windward, to the confusion of the Romans, who couldn't. And don't forget we're speaking of a time *before* Cuchulainn The Wanderer lived!''

''He wandered too?''

"He did. He's a Scottish hero too, from the time he helped Graham the Pict break through the Roman wall; and, of course, there was his love affair with the Pictish witch-queen Scathach." She giggled and added, "And herself without a stitch to wear, painted blue, with a cairn gorm jewel in her belly button. Who sleeps over there on that other pallet, Gaston?"

"We'd be in trouble if it was anyone more shapely. Ah, where are *you* bedded down this evening, Meabh?"

"Oh, I've a tent all to myself, since Sally Burnes and Pru Dorman are sharing one while Elvira, of course, sleeps with Himself."

She lowered her lashes and dimpled as she added, "I'm not used to sleeping alone in a tent surrounded by screaming wild animals. That may be why I've been lying awake for hours thinking about wandering, long-dead hero-gods and oaken ships with painted leather sails."

"And love affairs with barbarian queens painted blue?"

She flushed and said, "Perhaps. The point is that one needs *some* kind of a boat to get from Ulster to Scotland, too. And is it an accident our Irish legends place Tir nan Og, or the Fairyland of Eternal Youth, far out in the sunset sea, along with Fair Avalon, or the land of fruit the Vikings called 'Vineland'? We *know* the *Vikings* made it across. Who's to say Irish and Welsh legends of crossing the Main Ocean to a far green shore couldn't be based on fact?"

He shrugged and said, "Don't look at me. I wasn't there. What *difference* could it make at this late date?"

She looked hurt and said, "I'm a mythologist. Can't you see what an important paper I could present on the subject if only I could prove Cuchulainn of Ireland and Cuculcan of Central America and Mexico were one and the same? It would explain so much, Dick. Before three hundred A.D., the so-called Maya were just wandering food-gatherers, like the primitives still wandering about out there in the jungle. But say a sailing ship filled with people from a more civilized culture put in around here, somewhere, to show them a few tricks of the trade—"

He laughed and cut in, "Some tricks. Human sacrifice and a heathen god for every day of the year?"

She shrugged and said, "Well, Irish legend has cleaned Cuchulainn up a bit since Patrick of the Nine Hostages put out the fires of Beltane. The pagan Celts may have had some bloody notions as well as a full pantheon of somewhat grotesque gods. But they did know the use of metal, and how to build in stone. They knew how to fight, too, and, more important, how to organize scattered clans into real armies such as the Maya had—to the dismay of surrounding tribes, in the days of their glory."

Something plopped wetly on the canvas above them. So Captain Gringo said, "The days of Maya glory are long gone. But we're about to have a day, at least, of heavy rain. I've been expecting it since the trade winds died. I'd better get you back to your own tent before the old Maya god, Hurican, dumps Cuchulainn's Main Ocean on us."

She started to object. Then something clicked in her big, green innocent eyes and she let him help her to her bare feet. The night fires had died down to beds of barely glowing coals outside. But there was just enough ruby light to navigate by as he escorted Meabh to her own nearby tent. They just made it. They'd barely ducked inside when the shifting winds rained fire and salt down on the canvas they were under. He could barely make out her words as she trimmed her own oil lamp to a fainter glow and said, "Oh, you'll catch your death out there if you leave *now*, Dick! You'd better stay here till it lets up, don't you think?"

He thought they'd spent enough time sparring around when they both could see what the other found more interesting than comparative mythology, for God's sake. So he took her in his arms, said, "I'm not going anywhere," and kissed her not at all surprised lips.

She kissed back passionately, putting her back as well as tongue into it as she wrapped her little arms around him and tried to crush his ribs for some reason. But as he lowered her to her own sleeping pallet, she remembered she was supposed to say dumb things at times like these. So she asked him what he thought he was doing, even as she reached down to unfasten the only knot holding the front of her robe together.

He said, "Can't hear you. Raining too hard"—as he lay beside her on the bedding and cupped a perky breast in his free hand to kiss her some more. She moaned something silly with her soft lips crushed against his own as, having established she was a girl above the waist, he ran his hand down her trembling torso to part the red hair between her creamy thighs with friendly fingers. As he rocked the man in the boat for her, Meabh gasped, "Oh, please don't tease me, Darling!"

And then, since he couldn't figure out how to take his hand out of such pleasant surroundings without losing his advantage, Meabh helped solve the problem by unbuttoning his fly with her own free hand. As she reached in to explore him too, she suddenly flinched and gasped, "Mother of God! If you think you'll be putting such a feathered serpent indeed in *me*, you're sadly mistaken!"

But she was laughing as she said it, and spread her thighs in welcome as he rolled into the saddle, still fully clothed. Meabh hissed with pleased surprise as he entered her tight, warm love-flesh. But as he started moving in her, with her moving to meet his thrusts, she laughed roguishly and asked, "Do you always make love with your clothes and, Jesus, a shoulder holster on?"

He said, "Well, I left my *hat* behind, didn't I?" as he began to peel out of his clothes without dismounting or, thanks to the way she could move those trim hips, even stopping. She helped, enjoying the novelty of this approach to getting down to basics, and in no time at all they were both enjoying each other's naked bodies atop her terry-cloth robe and bedding. He was glad she hadn't trimmed the lamp all the way. Her petite pale body was beautiful to look at as well as beautiful to lay.

She came ahead of him. Then she came with him, and as they went limp in each other's arms, she sighed and protested, "Oh, whatever must you think of me now? I'll bet you think I came to your tent to seduce you, right?"

He said, "Sure, and I'm so glad. It saved me having to

come up with my own excuse to be alone with *you*. I was afraid you'd be bedded down with one of those two actresses."

She moved her hips teasingly as he soaked inside her and replied, "Why did you think I managed to get a private tent? But we're going to have to be very discreet about our relation, as far as the others are concerned. I'd just die if that fresh Sally Burnes had something like *this* to throw at me. Prudence Dorman's not catty, but Sally has a very cutting tongue in her mouth."

He started moving in her again as he said, "Let's see. Miss Dorman is the ash blonde and Sally Burnes is the one with light brown hair and the hots for that writer Blake, right?"

"I don't know if they've become *this* friendly yet. But they have been flirting outrageously since we all joined the professor. Why are we talking about other people at a time like this, Darling? Could you, ah, get in a little deeper?"

He could. He hooked an elbow under each of her naked knees and raised them, wide-spread, to enter her at an angle she seemed to find alarming. As her eyes opened wide and her rosebud lips made a little O of dismay, he eased off and asked if he was hurting her. She said, "No, it feels lovely, but this position is so . . . so obscene, if we were caught like this by anyone! Can't we have the lamp out, Dear?"

"Later. If I wanted to stop now, I couldn't. Nobody's going to catch us in any position, Honey. It's almost four in the morning and raining cats and dogs outside. Who'd be paying a social call to either tent at a time like this?"

"Won't your friend Gaston wonder where you are?"

"He's standing guard under a tree, or, knowing Gaston, he may decide to knock off early. But so what?"

"You're not going to tell him about us, are you?"

"Hell no, let him get his own girl. Don't worry. He's not nosy."

"But he'll surely think you must be with someone, if you're not with him, Darling?"

"I thought you didn't want to talk about other people at a time like this. Gaston and I hardly ever do this, and he's not my mother, either. What I might or might not be doing right now is none of his business, and *my* business is *comingggggg*!"

"Oh God, me too!" she moaned, digging her manicured nails into his bare back as she bowed her spine to take it all, hissing, "Yessssss!"

Then, just as they were coming back down from heaven, all hell broke loose outside!

Meabh stiffened in terror under him as the night was rent by the mad woodpecker chatter of a machine gun firing full automatic, close! Captain Gringo rolled off her, grabbed his .38 from the pile of clothing beside the pallet, and leaped to his feet to extinguish the lamp as he snapped, "Stay down. I mean it," and moved to open the tent flap just enough to see what was going on.

What was going on was that someone he couldn't see in the rain-swept darkness was pumping hot Maxim lead—lots of hot Maxim lead—at a target Captain Gringo also couldn't see. But he could see the muzzle flash firing inside the camp, at someone or something else inside the camp. So he trained his .38 on it and called out, "Knock that off! I won't say it twice!"

The muzzle of the machine gun swung his way, still firing as it sought out the sound of his voice with rapid-fire death. So Captain Gringo didn't yell again. He fired, aiming where the mystery gunner had to be on the far side of the muzzle flashes, then crabbed to one side in case he'd missed, fired again, and cut the other way to charge in as the Maxim fire ceased abruptly.

By this time the whole camp was up and making lots of noise, of course. Captain Gringo yelled, "Everybody hit the dirt and *stay* there!" as he moved in, spotted a dark form on the ground behind the barely visible machine gun tripod, and shot it again for luck.

It didn't move. He moved closer. Elvira Slade, who'd already established that rules and regulations didn't apply to her, ran up to him as he stood over the dark, dead form to demand, "What happened? Is that you, Dick? You . . . you're naked!"

He said, "Yeah, that's the way I usually get out of bed in a hurry. Are you and your husband okay?"

"Yes, but who was doing all that shooting just now?"

"I'll tell you when we have some light on the subject," he replied, calling out in Spanish, "I need a lantern over here poco tiempo!"

Three peones moved in from three directions, all three carrying oil lamps, bless them. As she got a better look at Captain Gringo's naked body, Elvira Slade, who was only wearing a short nightgown herself, said, "Heavens!" and turned to stare down at the fully dressed dead body staring up at them.

It was Blake. Captain Gringo wasn't as surprised as the others. There were lots of others now, despite his warning to stay down and back. One of them was Gaston, who took in the situation at a glance, took off his jacket, and handed it to Captain Gringo, saying, "Nice shooting, Dick. What was *he* shooting at?"

Captain Gringo wrapped the soggy jacket around his hips with a grateful nod as he replied, "Me, I think. Let's go see."

They did. They found their tent and just about everything in it riddled pretty good. But the hanging lamp was still burning, despite a .30-30 hole in its brass shade and missing glass.

Gaston bent to pick up the topsheet of his own sleeping roll and regarded the bullet holes in it with distaste, saying, "Merde alors, *I* never hit the species of idiot!"

Captain Gringo shrugged and replied, "Well, we'd established he had a nasty disposition, even before I decked him. He should have quit while he was ahead."

Gaston glanced over at Captain Gringo's shot-up bedding and said, "Oui, but where are your boots and pants, my naked youth? And how in the devil did he miss the rest of you?"

Captain Gringo reached up to douse the lamp and didn't answer. He couldn't. Everyone in camp seemed to be trying to crowd in with them at once, all asking questions at the same time. He couldn't answer them all at the same time, and even when he said, "Don't light that lamp, it's leaking!" one of the damned cameramen struck a match and lit it. Captain Gringo said, "Okay, let's all go outside." Then he saw his own boots and clothing had materialized as if by magic on his bedroll. Meabh O'Connor was standing to one side, her terry-cloth robe tied up sedately enough for Queen Victoria, and looking as if butter wouldn't melt in her mouth. Gaston was a quick thinker too; he herded everybody out, shouting, "Let the poor child put at least his pants on in private, hein?"

It worked. A few minutes later Captain Gringo had his boots, pants, and shirt on. It was still raining like hell, so they all wound up in Slade's nearby tent, save for the peones, who listened when they were told to go back to their own shelters or at least start breakfast fires.

Slade himself, slow-thinking as usual, was wide awake at last but still confused. Since he was the boss, Captain Gringo addressed his remarks to him as he explained, tersely, "Blake must have been good at holding a grudge. I don't know where he learned to man a machine gun. But he knew we had one among the supplies, and we all know why he was mad at me."

Little Sally Burnes sobbed, "Did you have to kill him, you brute?"

That was too dumb a question to answer. But the ash blonde, Prudence Dorman, said, "For heaven's sake, Sally, your Bruce was firing at him with a *machine* gun!"

"Pooh, he didn't *hit* anyone, did he? He was probably just trying to scare the big bully so he'd leave him alone!"

Elvira Slade looked at the younger woman thoughtfully and said, "You're fired, Sally." Then she turned to Captain Gringo and asked simply, "If we send some of our men back to Puerto Nogales with her, they can still catch up with us, can't they?"

He nodded. But Professor Slade blinked owlishly and asked his wife, "Why would we want to discharge the girl, Mommykins? She hasn't done anything, has she?"

Elvira sighed and said, "Huggy Bear, Mister Travis just had to shoot her boyfriend because her boyfriend went crazy and shot up the camp with a machine gun."

"I know, Mommykins. He must have been crazy. But is little Sally crazy, too?"

"She has to be if she's still making excuses for a homicidal maniac! I told you when you hired him I didn't like the way he showed so much white around the rims of his eyes, remember?"

"Yes, but we had to have a scriptwriter, Mommykins."

Meabh O'Connor said flatly, "*I* can write the titles for your film, Professor," and everyone but Captain Gringo looked surprised. He was beginning to get the distinct impression the little redhead from-a-clever-race-descended was a born opportunist who didn't hesitate to grab for any gold rings she spotted aboard the merry-go-round of life.

Elvira said, "We can talk about that later, Dear. Right now it's our Sally I'm concerned about."

Sally Burnes sobbed. "Oh, you can't leave me stranded in Puerto Nogales, Ma'am! I don't know a soul there! I don't even speak the language!"

Elvira arched an eyebrow at Captain Gringo and asked, "What do you think, Dick? It's your back."

He smiled thinly and said, "She's got a point about Puerto Nogales being no place to strand a nice girl alone, even if she *could* speak Spanish. Hardiman will have steamed away by now, and there's no telling how long it'll take us to get back there. I vote we take her with us."

Elvira said, "Well, as I said, it's your back, Dick. Do you think you could refrain from stabbing our guide in the back, Sally?"

"Oh please, Ma'am, I'll be good. I only said he was a brute. I never said I wanted to go anywhere *near* his back, or front! He's a big bully and he scares me!"

Elvira shrugged and said, "That's what I like to see in a child. Gratitude. All right, that's settled. What do we do now, Dick?"

Captain Gringo said, "We see that Blake's buried, clean the machine gun, and have breakfast. The night's about shot and everyone's up, right?"

"That's for sure. Can't we have breakfast first?"

He laughed and said, "If they can get the wood to burn in all that rain outside. You folks just have to get dressed. We'll see to the other minor details while the water's boiling."

The Slades were already in their own tent. So everyone else filed out to go get fully dressed in their own. Meabh had worked it so that she and Captain Gringo left about the same time. Outside, in the rainy dark, she clutched his arm and whispered, "You won't tell anybody about us, will you, Dear?"

He said, "Of course not. I always keep good things to myself. That was quick thinking on your part, getting my stuff back to my tent so fast, Doll."

She frowned and asked, "What are you talking about, Dick?" So he said, "My boots and, better yet, my pants. Didn't you sneak them from your tent into mine amid all the confusion, Meabh?"

"Oh, Mother of God, I was so confused I forgot all about them! You say they wound up in your tent anyway?"

"They sure did, just in the nick of time. But *you* didn't do it, *I* didn't do it, and *Gaston* didn't do it. He couldn't have known where they might be. . . . Did you ever get the feeling the Little People liked you, Irish?"

"No, and what on earth are you talking about, Dick?"

"Beats the hell out of me. But unless we're infested with helpful brownies all of a sudden, someone *else* around here sure did us one hell of a favor!"

Camped in a tropic rain forest, under a tropic rain, it was hard to say just when the sun came up. But by the time breakfast and the other chores were taken care of, it was light enough to trim the lamps if one left the tent flap open—and they had to, because the warm, gray rain was turning any unventilated space into a steambath.

When Captain Gringo's watch told him it was almost eight in the morning, he went to the Slade's tent to tell the professor and his wife, "Change of plans. We're breaking camp and pushing on."

Slade frowned and said, "Dick, it's raining out." So Captain Gringo said, "I noticed. That's one good reason to get moving. The new boots will break in sooner, walking in them wet. Any tracks they leave in the forest muck will wash away pretty good, too.''

Elvira said, ''But, Dick, you told us we'd spend most of the day here and push on after nightfall.''

He nodded and said, ''That's another reason. We're missing two porters, along with their mujeres and all the supplies they could carry with them. I'm hoping they were just simple thieves. Even so, they may gossip about us back in town. If anyone picks up the gossip, they won't be expecting us to leave this morning, and they'll expect us to follow the trail on the map. If we strike camp now, we could lose anyone trailing us and, better yet, nervous Mosquito Indians don't hunt in the rain. It messes up their bowstrings. So I figure a good twenty miles of undisturbed romping through the woods.''

He saw the look of dismay that passed between the middle-aged couple and settled for, ''Okay, fifteen miles.''

It was a white lie. Hardiman's map said the trading post they'd be making for was *over* twenty miles out, even beeline. But he knew that once he had his greenhorns within five miles of a night to be spent under tin roofing, warm and dry, he'd get another fast five miles out of them. It was an old drill sergeant's trick that always worked with boots that hadn't been properly broken in. That was why it was an old trick.

Slade got up and said, ''Very well. I'd better have my cameraman, Dillon, set up to crank a shot of us moving out. I wish there was more light.''

He left, leaving Captain Gringo and Elvira alone. He asked her, ''Are we going to do that a lot, Ma'am?'' and she said, ''Of course. There's no money in exploring if you don't bring something back you can charge people to see, is there?''

''If you say so. I'd better get cracking myself, Miss Elvira.''

But she said, ''Stay awhile, Dick. What's your hurry? We've never really gotten the chance to talk alone.''

He didn't ask what she wanted to talk about. Her eyes

glowed with lust, and they creeped him, even knowing what great legs she had. He said he'd be proud to have a long chat with her at a more convenient time, and she said she'd hold him to that promise, purring like a cat in heat as she did so. That gave him something else to worry about as he ducked out to shout the orders needed to strike the tents and lash everything together. He wondered if it had been the late Blake with her the night before. That would account for being in the market for new slap and tickle, as she obviously was.

But Blake wouldn't work so good for several reasons. Guys who'd just been laid, good, seldom felt like killing anybody at the moment, and Blake hadn't just been in a sullen mood. He'd been mad with rage he had to have nursed into a *killing* rage, with a bottle and lots of talking to himself. The guy hadn't planned worth a damn. Anyone with sense would have known that he'd have never gotten away with such an open attack. The guy who'd been banging old Elvira when her husband woke up to look for her had played it cool. So, yeah, it had to be somebody else, and old Elvira just felt the need for more sex than one husband and one lover on the side could offer a woman of her appetites. The idea was sort of awe-inspiring. But if there was one dame attached to the expedition he didn't want to mess with, she was it.

He knew who was getting Meabh. He wondered who, if anyone, was getting the blonde, Pru, or the little brown-haired gal who didn't like him. He wondered why he cared. The redhead was more than enough for any sensible guy right now. He wouldn't have made a play for *her* if she hadn't given him such a bright green light with her big green eyes.

But the damage was done, and it probably wouldn't cause any trouble if the redhead meant what she'd said about kiss and tell. He saw one of the tents still standing alone with its tent flap closed. He called a peon over and asked how come. The Honduran said, "The two Yanqui men inside say they are not ready for to leave yet, Señor."

Captain Gringo grunted in annoyance and moved over to

the tent, calling out, "Come on, you guys, rise and shine. You're holding up the parade!"

Then, as he opened the flap and stuck his head in, he saw that the lab man Ferris was holding the balls of Simpson in his cupped hands as he sucked his dong.

Ferris, on his knees with his eyes closed, paid no attention. But Simpson gasped. "Jesus, don't you ever knock, you bastard!"

Captain Gringo didn't say what he thought either of *them* was. He just said, "Sorry, Girls. But make it snappy, will you? We've got most of the other tents struck, and you'll have all the time you want for that stuff later tonight."

He ducked back out, grimacing. He walked through the rain, now not as heavy, to where Gaston was sitting on a pile of packs smoking a wet cigar under his dripping hat brim. Captain Gringo asked, "Are those the packs we're supposed to drop off with the trader, Breslin?" and Gaston said, "Oui. I still think we should have the machine gun a bit more easy to get at, should we need it."

The taller American shrugged and said, "Let's hope we don't need it, then. Breslin's expecting it in mint condition, and I had a time getting it back to any condition at all after that asshole fired a full belt through a cold barrel in one burst. I've regreased it good. But packing it all day exposed to this drizzle could sure bring out any spots I missed. Automatic fire's not much use in a hit-and-run jungle fight in any case."

Gaston sighed and said, "Please, I just ate breakfast, Dick. Some of our porters are of the opinion the local Indians are très restless this season, too."

"Oh? Did they say what tribe?"

"Oui, *all* of them! One gathers the local warlord, Don Nogales, has been slave-raiding. That is one reason I was able to recruit so many unemployed mestizos. One need not pay a Spanish-speaking mestizo *much* to pick bananas. But one must pay him more than one need pay a kidnapped Indian child, hein?"

Captain Gringo frowned and said, "Chattel slavery is

illegal in Honduras these days. It says so right in their constitution.''

"Oui, I've read it. But who *else* reads constitutions down this way or, to be fair, in some of your adorable United States? The Nogales family has been expanding its banana business. The so-called trees only take a year or so to grow, and they grow between stumps, with little expert cultivation, once one clears more jungle. Jungle-reared Indians are not good for *skilled* labor, but, pound for pound, they are healthier and hence stronger than pobrecitos who grew up on peon food and wages, so—"

"It's just plain stupid," Captain Gringo cut in, adding, "To become boss and to have their own shipping port named after them, the Nogales clan has to have been in this neck of the woods awhile. How long could even powerful planters get away with abusing the local tribes in defiance of their own central government?"

"Our porters tell me they just started, less than a year ago, when the old Don Nogales died and his powerful place was taken by a son who'd just returned from Harvard Business School."

"They teach slave-raiding at *Harvard*?"

"Mais non, but they must have taught him bookkeeping, and as I just said, slaves work for less than the most downtrodden peasant. What did you think that thwarted revolution was all about, Dick? The plotters were probably not worried about the welfare of despised Indians, but worried about their own unemployment. It is très hard to find a job when the only major industry in the province is not hiring, hein?"

"Yeah, but the local establishment had to send for the army to put down the revolt, and the army works for the central government and . . . right, the local military commander's on the take. It still sounds like this Don Nogales is doing things the needlessly complicated way, though. If I was in the banana business, I'd just take the dough it takes to bribe at least a whole mess of officers and use it to pay my help."

"Oui, so would I, Dick. But, then, neither of us are dedicated sons of the bitch. Politics would not be so hectic down here, and soldiers of fortune like you and me would not find such a ready market for our skills, if the people running things were not such simple-minded greedy pigs. The average Hispanic peon, like the average man everywhere, is content with simple food and shelter and perhaps a few of life's simple luxuries. But when one has been raised from the cradle to consider anyone so poor he has to work some sort of lower animal, one would rather spend money to keep him in his place than to pay the poor brute a living wage, hein?''

''Jesus, I ask what time it is and you tell me how to build the clock.''

Gaston looked injured and replied, ''If you don't want to hear about wheels within wheels, do not ask about what's going on.''

Captain Gringo nodded and said, ''You're right. It sounds too complicated for sane people to worry about. Let's get this show on the road. Getting these smuggled arms to Breslin and leading Slade deep enough into the woods to convince him he's on a wild-goose chase will be complicated enough.''

Getting all the gear packed and everybody ready to move out was more chaotic than complicated. But at last he had the expedition moving out again. All but two of them. For some reason, Dillon, the professor's cameraman, was recording a pretty dull-looking scene on film as the blonde actress, Prudence Dorman, stood by him and his tripod giving advice on camera angles as Dillon cranked the Edison-Eastman box.

Captain Gringo didn't comment or even stop as he passed them. If they couldn't figure out they were supposed to catch up when they finished whatever they thought they were doing, tough shit.

Under the dark canopy, deeper into the rain forest, the rain wasn't coming down in a steady drizzle. The treetops acted as countless funnels to pour countless steady streams one could almost walk between. Now and again a wind shift, unfelt at ground level, dumped an unexpected bucket of piss-warm water on someone's head; but when it wasn't raining up there, the parrots and monkeys shit on you a lot, so it evened out.

Such wildlife as there was in deep jungle naturally sheltered itself invisibly while it rained. Almost nothing big enough to matter lived on the soggy jungle floor they were slogging their way across between the massive trees. Nothing a deer or tapir would eat could grow in such dense shade. Some of the mushrooms they stepped on were bigger than tennis balls. But they mostly walked on a black, spongy carpet of rotting twigs and fallen leaves. Captain Gringo's own well-broken-in mosquito boots were soaked through and squishing on his big feet. He knew the soaking would do wonders for the blisters and new boots of the greenhorns, whether it felt comfortable or not. He walked them a good hour, then called a trail break, yelling loudly, "Smoke if you gottem, but no fires. We're only taking ten!"

The porters dumped their loads and sat on them. The whites found out, the hard way, one disadvantage of not carrying one's own stuff on safari.

He saw Pru Dorman and Sally Burnes making for a mossy fallen log to rest their pretty asses on and called out, "I wouldn't do that if I were you, girls."

The ash blonde stopped, staring at him with a puzzled expression. Sally ignored him and sat down on the log. Then she sprang up, screaming like a banshee as she batted at her skirts with both hands. Her blonde chum gasped and said, "Sally, you've got ants all over you! *Big* ones!"

Captain Gringo wondered what else was new. There were logs one could sit on in a jungle and there were logs one shouldn't. One was supposed to look them over first. He saw the blonde was helping the other girl brush the driver ants off her ass. So he moved on. At least, so far, nobody had sat on a bushmaster. It was probably only a question of time. But, what the hell, they had plenty of snake-bite kits in the professor's medical supplies.

He hadn't known they'd brought along their own snakes, though, until he saw the cameraman, Dillon, coming his way with the camera tripod over one shoulder as he dragged what looked like a dead python behind him like a pull toy, by its tail.

Dillon said, "I want a shot of you struggling with this deadly boa, Dick."

Captain Gringo laughed and said, "No, you don't. That's not a boa. The markings are all wrong for this part of the world. Where in the hell did you get that, and what is it, stuffed or rubber?"

Dillon said, "Rubber. Picked it up at a prop shop in New York, in case we couldn't find real snakes this big down here."

"Snakes that big and bigger they've got. But not in this sort of country. Anaconda hang around rivers and swamps. Boas live way up in the trees. They eat birds and monkeys a lot."

Dillon shrugged and said, "Whatever. Who's going to know the diff, once we pose you right with this critter? You'd better take off that hat and jacket. Gun rig, too. If you were packing a gun when this thing jumped you, you could just shoot it instead of fighting for your life in its coils, right?"

"Wrong. I've got more than one reason for not wanting to be photographed, and if I *did* want my picture taken, it wouldn't be in such a ridiculous pose. I thought this was supposed to be a *scientific* expedition, Dillon."

The older, more jaded-looking man failed to look defensive as he answered calmly, "I'm not a scientist. I'm a pro working for a percentage of the gross. If we don't take interesting travel films, nobody will come to *see* them. Get it?"

"I'm beginning to. Whose idea was it to have me, of all people, fighting for my life in the coils of a rubber snake?"

Dillon said, "Meabh O'Connor's writing a new script. She seems to think you're the hero. Great white hunter and all that shit. If you're camera shy, do you think that little Frenchman would fight this thing for me?"

"Don't even ask. Gaston fights with his feet. Get one of the porters or, better yet, one of the prettier native girls."

Dillon grinned and said, "Hey, that's a great idea! Thanks! In educational travel films, it's okay to show tits if they're *dark* enough!"

The cameraman and his prop python went away. Captain Gringo found a log that *hadn't* been claimed as a rainy-day bivouac by driver ants, and sat down to wet his tail while he gave his legs a break. He'd just managed to light a claro with a waterproof match that needed lots of encouragement when the lab man Simpson joined him for a word or two in private. Captain Gringo didn't invite him to sit beside him. So Simpson stood there, sort of sheepishly, and said, "Look, about what you caught Ferris doing, back there . . ."

Captain Gringo blew smoke out his nostrils in annoyance and said, "I didn't catch anyone doing anything *alone*, Pal. But don't stew about it. I'm a live-and-let-live guy."

"Oh? Then you understand how other guys might have . . . ah, needs?"

"Don't push your luck. I'd stick mine in a pig first. It wouldn't make me feel so silly saying good-bye afterwards."

"Look, Travis, Ferris is a queer, as you saw. But *I'm* not."

"Do we have to argue about it, Simpson? I know some guys get a kick out of baiting queers. I don't. I don't have to fight any secret desires, and, what the hell, it cuts down on the competition for dames. I said I wasn't going to say anything about it. So why are *you* saying so much about it?"

"I just want to get it straight with you, Travis. I wouldn't want you thinking I was a fairy."

Captain Gringo shrugged and said, "I haven't been thinking much about you one way or the other. Everybody looks a little silly when they're coming. So you just come your way and let me come mine and we'll say no more about it."

"You won't tell any of the others?"

"Jesus, what a secretive bunch you all seem to be. I said I wouldn't. Do you want it in blood?"

"I was hoping you'd take that attitude, Travis. You're okay. If there's any favor I can ever do you, just ask."

Captain Gringo didn't want a blow-job. At least, not from another guy. So he chuckled and said, "Maybe you can invite Gaston and me the next time you show those stag films, if you've got any I haven't seen."

"Stag films?" Simpson answered with a convincingly innocent expression.

Captain Gringo said, "Come on, you were using the projector in the tent you share with Ferris last night, weren't you?"

Simpson said, "Not exactly. Ferris has other, ah, more interesting tricks. But I just can't make it that way, with the lights on. We loaned the projector to Sally and Pru last night, as a matter of fact. Pru is interested in the new art of motion pictures and . . . Did you say *stag* films? Most of the film we've brought with us is still raw stock. Where would anyone get stag films in the middle of a jungle?"

"Just kidding. And we're a long way from the middle of this jungle. So let's get everyone moving again."

He stood and walked away from Simpson, calling out, "Everybody up!" in both English and Spanish. As the expedition lined up to move out again, he passed the blonde and brunette. He couldn't help asking Sally if she still had ants in her pants. So she called him a brute again.

As he led the way at the head of the column, checking his pocket compass from time to time and compensating for his own natural drift to the left that he'd discovered long ago— the hard way—in Apache country, Captain Gringo tried not to think of ants in Sally's pants. He had a romantic redhead back there just waiting for the sun to set again, and if he wasn't careful, old Elvira was going to make him fight for his virtue the moment she could corner him alone. But it was sort of interesting to know the only two dames left over were watching dirty moving pictures together instead of doing it right with any of the other guys attached to the expedition.

He knew whom the professor was sleeping with, half her time. Blake was dead. Ferris and Simpson were sleeping with each other, no matter how Simpson tried to define his sex life. That left the cameraman, Dillon, and the four guys he still knew little about; Morrison, Baldwin, Parsons, and Wayne. Morrison and Parsons were both good-looking enough to be actors, and for a scientific expedition this was sure turning out to be a melodrama. He couldn't narrow it down any closer. Hell, when a horny old bawd was as horny as old Elvira, he couldn't narrow it down at all. She hadn't been cheating with Gaston, and Blake had acted like a guy who hadn't been getting any lately. But the guy inside the tent with her could have been anyone else, save for the two homosexuals. He hadn't heard the guy's voice. So, hell, she could have even been with a native and . . . no, that wouldn't work. The porters hadn't been issued tents, and Elvira hadn't been cheating on her husband in the tent she shared with *him*.

He put the matter aside. It was uncomfortable to walk with a dawning hard-on. He knew better than to ask himself why thinking about old Elvira should give any sensible man an erection. Forbidden fruit was like that; that was probably why nuts like the emperor Nero wound up in bed with their own sisters, given a whole empire filled with willing slave girls to choose from. Human nature was a pain in the ass.

The day wore on and on, more tedious than filled with anything worth remembering. The rain let up about noon. It didn't make much difference. The trees would go on dripping for hours, and the overhead canopy kept the sun from heating the jungle floor enough to slow them down. He gave them a lunch break near a sluggish stream of tea-brown water winding wearily between the buttress roots, too narrow to cut its own slot of sunlight.

But a few hundred yards upstream where a giant mahogany had given up the ghost after hundreds of years of growing and taken a few acres of younger trees down with it in its fall, the cameraman, Dillon, found a patch of sunlit space that looked a lot more like his idea of a jungle suitable for filming.

Actually, it was an awful mess. Dillon had to get some natives to mâchete tons of wet, squishy weeds and sprawling vines out of the way before he had a sort of sunlit stage with a backdrop of what looked like giant celery armed with thorns and laced together with glandular grapevines. As the others, including the natives, watched, Dillon set up his camera, consulted the script, and said, "All right, Morrison. You and Sally get out there by that big black stump. Take your hat off and let your hair down, Sally."

The actors started to obey. Then Captain Gringo gasped, shoved the brown-haired Sally at the male actor, and drew his .38. Morrison looked more like a jungle explorer than he really was. He just stood there, gaping, when Sally fell past him to land flat on her face as Captain Gringo fired.

She rolled over, sat up red with rage, and gasped, "You crazy ape!"

None of the other whites could even guess why he'd done it, either. So there was more than a little uneasy muttering behind him as the actor, Morrison, helped Sally to her feet again, saying, "Be careful. *I* think he's crazy, too, and he's holding a *gun* in his hand!"

Captain Gringo snorted in disgust and moved forward into the weed stubble as he holstered his .38, bent over, and hauled out an awesome length of dark, mottled snake, still twitching even though it was missing most of its head now.

He held it aloft, its bloody, mangled head still almost touching the ground as it bled some more, and said, "This is what you call a bushmaster. It's related to our own rattlers. But, as you may have just noticed, bushmasters don't have rattles. So they can't tell you to watch your step. You're supposed to *look* where you're stepping in heavy underbrush down here."

Sally stared for a few seconds of breathless horror at the monstrous creature she'd almost put a dainty foot on, and then she swayed, eyes glazed, and Captain Gringo warned Morrison, "Grab her. She's blacking out!"

Morrison did, still staring stupidly until Elvira and Meabh moved in to take charge of the fainting girl and sit her down to inhale some of the older woman's smelling salts. Captain Gringo wondered where she'd been carrying it. Old Elvira was full of surprises.

Having discovered the perils of staging dramatics in fresh-cleared brush, Dillon settled for a panning shot of the otherwise empty salad bowl as Meabh took shorthand notes on what they might have to say about it later.

When it was time to move out again, Captain Gringo took advantage of the excitement, knowing they could all walk a little faster without noticing it, now that their blood was circulating pretty good.

Aside from the few distractions, they were making better time than he'd anticipated. The route he'd chosen was level and more free of fallen timber or swampy stretches than lots of jungle he'd seen. He still had to give them occasional trail breaks, of course. He told them they were stopping once an hour. It was actually once every hour and a half. Those extra thirty minutes added up to about two extra miles per break at the pace he was setting. He, Gaston, and probably the natives, could have moved faster in such open jungle. But, for greenhorns, they were moving far better than expected.

During one of the trail breaks, he was hunkered down with his back against a buttress root, consulting his maps, when Sally Burnes joined him. She dropped to her folded knees, since it wasn't ladylike to hunker, even though the ground was black and squishy. She said, "Dick, I think I owe you an apology."

He said, "No you don't. I'd have been annoyed as hell if you'd shot my lover and pushed me on my face, too."

She lowered her lashes and said, "Bruce Blake wasn't my lover. I just knew him better than I knew you, or thought I did. You know, of course, you saved my life back there?"

"Sure, that's why I pushed you on your face. Don't make it awkward for yourself, Honey. I hired on as a guide, not to win any popularity contests. I know I make some people nervous. Some people rub *me* the wrong way, too, present company excused. You're a pretty girl. You just proved you're a lady too. So don't make yourself uncomfortable trying to be nice to the hired help. War's over, okay?"

She smiled, but still looked uncomfortable as she replied, "I know it's silly of me to feel uneasy around you, Dick. I don't even know why I do. You haven't done anything to me. You've been very helpful to everyone, in your own tough way. But . . . would you mind if I asked you why you act so tough, Dick?"

He shrugged and put the map away as he reached for a smoke, saying, "It's a tough world, Sally. I didn't make the rules. I'm just stuck with 'em."

"You've been bitterly hurt, haven't you?"

He lit his claro before he smiled crookedly and said, "Everyone gets bitterly hurt if they live long enough. Down here, living long enough can be the problem. The natives won't work for a guy they have down as a softy. If I wasn't a little hard on the rest of you, we'd be about ten miles back, right now. Don't waste time trying to figure me out, Sally."

He was too polite to add he couldn't figure her out, either.

She sure didn't look like a girl who enjoyed watching Chinamen eat French ladies. But then, when French ladies were out in public with their clothes on, Queen Victoria expected *them* to look innocent, too.

Before the brown-haired Sally could delve deeper into his soul, the redhead, Meabh, came over to join them, smiling sweetly as her green eyes shot daggers. Meabh ignored Sally as she said, "Oh, there you are, Dick. I've got an idea for a scene we could shoot when there's time. Do you think you could find us any quicksand?"

He laughed and said, "I hope not. Quicksand's fairly rare, thank God, even along sandy streambeds. Who were you planning to push in quicksand, Irish?"

Meabh looked right at Sally, but said, "Nobody, really. But if we had one of our porters sort of get down on his knees in wet sand—boggy muck or something—then threw him a rope just in time . . ."

"Yeah, Dillon could probably make that look pretty dramatic. And an audience that will buy a rubber Asiatic python as a Central American boa would probably buy anything. There's a jungle trading post ahead, on the banks of a fairly wide stream. It's a little out of our way. But we can swing over that way and Dillon should find any number of places to set up."

Meabh said, "Oh good, I'll tell him. He's done nothing but complain about the uninteresting scenery so far. Coming, Sally dear?"

Sally must not have wanted to argue. She nodded, rose, and brushed off her skirt, saying something about talking more about it later. Meabh was too much a lady herself to ask how Sally intended to manage that without getting killed.

As the two girls moved away together through the trees, Gaston joined Captain Gringo, hunkered down, and said, "Eh bien, you look unusually pleased with yourself all of a sudden, Dick. Please don't tell me why. I saw them just now. What do you do, put something in their coffee?"

"I think I just put a bug in Professor Slade's ear. I've been wondering just how we were going to excuse taking them out of the way to Breslin's trading post. Now they'll think it's their idea. I'll be glad to get rid of the extra guns and ammo. It should make the traveling lighter.''

Gaston frowned and said, ''It depends on who we meet, deeper in this très fatigué spinach, non?''

He'd been hoping to make the trading post by sundown. Thanks to the easier-than-expected going, it was more like five-thirty when he called a halt, gathered the straw bosses of the porters together with Slade and the male whites, and said, ''Gaston and I are going on ahead to scout the trading post. The map says it's less than a mile away, that way. Meanwhile, I want the rest of you to pile the supplies in a circle, break out the extra rifles, and make sure nobody but us gets inside until we come back.''

Slade frowned and asked, ''Why did you lead us here if you expect such a cool welcome from those jungle traders, Travis?''

Captain Gringo said, ''It was your idea to come this way at all. I *don't* expect Breslin's men to do anything but offer us some canned goods at ridiculous prices. But trading posts in Indian country trade with Indians. The local Indians seem to be pissed off about something, and, Jesus, do I have to draw pictures on blackboards, Professor?''

Slade said, ''Oh, right, Indians mad at whites would expect to lay for them near a white trading post.'' He turned to Dillon and asked, ''Don't you think you should set up both cameras, Bill?''

Dillon said he'd already thought of it, adding, ''Pru Dorman can crank the other one if need be. She's pretty good with the shutter speed now. I've been letting her practice with no stock in the older camera.''

Captain Gringo couldn't have cared less who was going to take moving pictures if they were in any trouble. He signaled Gaston and muttered, ''Let's go.''

Dillon said, ''Wait. I'd better get a shot of you two moving out. Could you sort of walk in a crouch, rifles at port arms?''

Captain Gringo said, "Later. With any luck, there won't be anything ahead worth crouching at."

He was wrong. But he didn't know it until he and Gaston were almost a mile from the others, with sunlight streaming down on the river ahead. He said, "There's the Rio Verde. So where's the fucking trading post?"

Gaston said, "Upstream or downstream, of course. Not even you can hit a pinpoint on the map by dead reckoning, Dick."

The tall American asked, "Wanna bet? If the streamside almost dead ahead hadn't been cleared, and kept cleared, we wouldn't be looking at such a gap in the riverside greenery. But I've never seen a trading post compound with nothing *standing* in it before. Let's move in. Watch out for other surprises."

"Merde alors, tell a gypsy how to steal chickens. Wait, do you smell what I smell, Dick?"

Captain Gringo sniffed again, grimaced, and said, "Yeah, I can hear the flies too now. Come on. Nobody alive would be hanging around here now. Even murderers have feelings."

They advanced to the trading-post clearing. The clearing was still there, covered with patches of mud and burnt grass. The four buildings of the compound had been burnt to the ground, too. Smoke was still curling out from under a pile of scorched corrugated metal roofing. As they moved closer, brushing the blue-bottle flies away from their faces with their free hands, Gaston pointed at a charred human hand clutching a charred arrow as it projected from under the edge of the fallen roofing. Gaston moved to lift it. Captain Gringo said, "Don't. It's obvious he needs help less than I need to keep my last meal down."

Gaston said, "Eh bien, he seems to have pulled that arrow out of himself as he went down. But I agree it did him little good. Do you suppose the others are under there with him?"

Captain Gringo pointed with his chin at what could have been taken for the tracks of a small farm tractor at the water's edge and said, "Any that fell in the open were dragged into the river by the crocs last night, or the night before. From the smell, I'd say they were hit no more than forty-eight hours ago, right?''

Gaston shook his head and said, ''Mais non. Make it twenty-four and trust an old observer of battlefields south of the Tropic of Cancer. Decay progresses très dramatique out in the open sun like this.''

''Okay, screw figuring out just when they were hit. The question before the house now is Who hit 'em? That doesn't look like a Mosquito arrow to me.''

Gaston nodded and said, ''That is because it is Chorti. Mosquito and Pipil favor longer arrows of reed. That one's hardwood. Just long enough for a stout shortbow. May I be excused for the rest of the afternoon?''

Captain Gringo pursed his lips and said, ''You've got a point. If the Maya speaking Chorti are on the warpath, this may not be the time to approach them about Maya ruins.''

''Oui, and if there are any Maya ruins for miles, they will of course be in Chorti country. I wonder why our jolly slave-raider Don Nogales bothered Chorti, of all people.''

Captain Gringo said, ''Maybe because most Maya speakers still know a little about slash-and-burn agriculture. Maybe they were mad at this bunch for some other reason entirely. I still haven't figured out why this Breslin guy needs machine guns, for God's sake, to trade with Indians.''

''If he is under all that scorched tin at the moment, he waited too long for *any* sort of extra weaponry! Perhaps he was slave-raiding, too?''

Captain Gringo shook his head and said, ''It won't work. Hardiman was a knockaround guy. His pal Breslin is or was a knockaround guy. But if they'd been in good with the local warlord, they wouldn't have needed us to run their guns, right?''

''Eh bien. Mais, in that case, why would the Indians want to attack people running guns to *enemies* of the Don Nogales they are so annoyed at? Could not they see which side of their bread the butter was on?''

Captain Gringo shrugged and said, ''If people always saw which side of their bread the butter was on, history would be less interesting. How the hell should *I* know what a scared illiterate taught to fear all strangers might or might not have on his pagan mind? I told you how tough it used to be to talk sense to Apache, in my misspent youth. You could tell 'em they were acting suicidal and they'd do it anyway. And, shit, I sort of understand *Apache*! I'm out of my league with long-lost Maya who were acting sort of weird even before their empire fell apart a thousand years ago."

"Don't look at me. You were the one who shacked up with that Maya witch and survived. All in all, I think our best bet would be to avoid any contact with them at all, non?"

Captain Gringo said, "When you're right, you're right. Let's go tell Slade and the others it's time to get our asses in gear and out of here."

Professor Slade didn't want to turn back. Or, if he did, his wife wouldn't let him. It was Elvira's idea to film the massacre site, adding they could flesh the scene out with what she called a stock shot. As Dillon panned the scene with his hand-cranked camera, Captain Gringo asked her what she meant and she explained, "We'll splice in an Indian war dance before we show the burned-out trading post. Then we'll splice in a victory dance."

"How do you figure on shooting those scenes, Miss Elvira?"

"We don't have to. We already have stock shots, shot by someone else, of a Hopi snake dance and some Navajo praying for rain or something. We'll decide as we edit which dance is which."

Captain Gringo laughed incredulously and said, "None of the tribes down here look anything like Navajo or Hopi, Miss Elvira." And she just shrugged and asked, "Who's going to know? How many people have ever seen *any* kind of Indian, dancing or not? If we can get real pictures of real Central American Indians, so much the better. But you'll have to admit that scene over there by the river is pretty dull without any action scenes to frame it."

Before he could answer, they both heard more than one woman scream. He turned to see that Dillon had gotten Simpson and Ferris to turn over the corrugated roofing for a better view of what lay under it. One of the more feminine screams had come from Ferris.

There were over a dozen bodies exposed to the sun now. They were not in great shape. Their clothing and most of their skin had been reduced to black char. Their heads were all missing. What was left was bloated and crawling with maggots. They didn't smell nice, either. But Dillon went on cranking as he chortled, "Now that's more like it! *This'll* make a *great* shot!"

Everyone else was backing away, trying not to gag. Sally Burnes didn't try hard enough. She made it to a tree near Captain Gringo, leaned against it, sobbing, and threw up all down the front of her whipcord skirt.

Captain Gringo went over to her, took her gently by one arm, and said, "Come on. We'd better head upstream, out of sight, and I'll wash that off for you before it sticks."

Neither she nor anyone else saw fit to argue as he hauled her away from the grisly photography session. He led her around the bend, sat her on a dry, sun-baked log near the water's edge, and took out his own pocket kerchief as she just went on bawling with hands covering her face. He hunkered down, swished the kerchief in the river, wrung it out, then swished it some more. He'd wiped his wet dong with it a couple of times in the recent past and wanted to *start* fresh, at least.

He knelt before her, holding the hem of her skirt taut from her knees down as he sponged the vomit with the kerchief. Sally sort of peeked out between her fingers at him and said, "Oh, you're going to ruin that poor kerchief, Dick."

He said, "No, I'm not. There's plenty of water in that river. It's a little acid from all the woods it's been running through, too. Indian women manage to do their laundry pretty good, without soap, in acid water."

"Brrr, don't mention Indians to me, Dick! Did you see what Indians did to those poor people back there?"

"Yeah. I'm still trying to figure out what somebody must

have done to the *Indians*! It's dumb to hit a trading post, even when you're on the warpath. You can always find someone else to put an arrow in. But after you calm down, you still need somewhere to buy your matches, salt, and stuff.''

"Nobody will ever be able to buy anything from *that* trading post again! Why did they cut their heads off? Wasn't killing them bad enough?''

He went on sponging as he frowned thoughtfully and replied, "I'm still working on that. I know Pipil and Mosquito don't go in for head-hunting. Don't know as much about Chorti and Sambo. But the only head-hunting Indians I've ever run into were Jivaro, way to the south in Amazonia.''

"My God, you've tangled with headhunters and you still have your *head*?''

He chuckled fondly and said, "I never had to fight the Jivaro. They're not bad kids if you can manage to talk to them before anyone gets hurt.''

He was able to reach the water with his kerchief without getting up. So he did so, adding as he swished it in the shallows, "I think we got most of your lunch. Better rinse it down with clean water once for luck. We've still got a little sun. Stay out in it if you want that cloth to dry before sundown. You may have noticed it sets poco tiempo, once it decides to. They don't go in for lingering sunsets this far south.''

She'd recovered some of her poise by now. She thanked him and added, "You certainly have been around, Dick. You never did get around to telling me how you came to be a—?''

"Banana republic bum?'' he answered with a crooked smile, adding: "It's a long, dull story, Sally. You wouldn't be interested.''

"Oh, but I *am*!'' she insisted, leaning forward to place a hand on his shoulder and saying: "I may be just an actress to you. But I've always been interested in other people's emotions, despite what you may have heard about my profession being filled with egomaniacs. I can tell by the way you talk that you were raised by gentlefolk and that you've been to college.''

"West Point,'' he corrected without thinking. Then,

remembering he was supposed to be a professional guide rather than a soldier of fortune, he added, "There wasn't much opportunity in a peacetime army. So I came down this way with my engineering degree to see if they needed help with the Panama Canal. The Canal's been stalled since the French syndicate that started it went bust, and Colombia won't let anyone else even start unless they're willing to make every petty official in Colombia a millionaire. Meanwhile, I gotta eat. So now you know as much about me as I do, Sally. Satisfied?"

"Not really. I can't help feeling you're holding back on me, Dick. You've had a tragic past. A woman can always tell."

The redhead must have had women's intuition, too. She came around the bend, calling out, "Oh, there you two are. I'm sorry to break this touching scene up, boys and girls, but the professor is holding a council of war, and Dick, at least, is needed back at the clearing."

Captain Gringo rose, helped Sally to her feet, and held her hand as he led her back to the others, if only to teach the redhead not to be so possessive. That was the trouble with dames. Let a guy throw a little friendly fucking to them, and they acted as if they owned him.

Sally didn't want to look at more headless bodies. As soon as she found out some of the others had headed back to their camp a mile away, she said she'd wait there. As soon as Captain Gringo was alone with the redhead, Meabh grabbed his arm and demanded, "Are you trying to make time with that mousy little bitch, you bastard?"

He smiled down at her and said, "Don't put ideas in my head. And don't act so bitchy if you want to stay friends with me, Red. Come on. Let's see what's on the professor's little pointed head."

They circled the charred ruins to join the group clustered around a pair of dugout canoes beached just downstream. As they approached, Slade spotted them and called out, "We seem to have a mutiny on our hands here, Dick."

The actor Morrison said, "Mutiny my Auntie Fanny Adams!

There was nothing in the contract we signed about getting our heads cut off by howling savages!''

Captain Gringo stared thoughtfully down at the canoes and said, ''Yeah, the guys who hit the trading post went *up-stream*. You could load at least a dozen frightened people or at least half a dozen more sensible ones, and the supplies they'd need to float back to the coast, in these dugouts, I guess.''

He caught Gaston's eye on the far side of the crowd and asked, ''How far is the mouth of the Verde from Puerto Nogales, Gaston?''

The Frenchman said, ''A good day's swampy stroll. With native help, they'd make it. It would not be a good idea to try it without someone who can tell a snake from a mangrove root before he or she steps over it, hein?''

Slade's wife, Elvira, snapped, ''Nobody is about to desert us now that we're almost *there,* damn it!''

One of the other hired actors, Wayne, asked Captain Gringo, ''*Are* we almost there, Travis?'' So Captain Gringo shook his head and said, ''We're not halfway there if there even *is* a there.'' Then he turned to the Slades and said, ''We can't get everybody in two canoes, and following the river back to the coast would be heading home the dumb way when you have guides. But I think we should *all* be heading back about now. This is getting to be just too big a boo.''

Slade just looked worried. Elvira snapped, ''Nonsense. We can't turn back now.''

Captain Gringo said, ''Sure you can. I don't think there's one Indian to worry about to the east. The ones who hit this trading post should be waiting somewhere to the west, where you keep making dumb remarks about *going*!''

''What of it? We have plenty of guns, don't we?''

''Yeah, just like the traders here did.''

''Don't be silly. They didn't have that machine gun,'' she insisted as her husband blinked and said, ''I've been meaning to ask about that machine gun. I don't remember purchasing any machine gun. We seem to have brought along more military rifles and ammunition than I ever ordered, too.''

Captain Gringo shrugged and said, ''Don't look at me. I

was sort of surprised when Blake hauled the Maxim out to smoke up my tent, too. Let's not worry about that now. The guys who attacked this post were probably Chorti. That's the only Maya-speaking tribe in this part of Honduras. Ergo, any Maya ruins you could hope to photograph are just out of reach at the moment."

He'd committed a tactical error. Elvira pursed her lips and sort of hissed through them, saying in a most determined manner, "We'll just have to make friends with them or shoot them, then. Either way, we can't turn back before we've shot those lost ruins!"

Morrison snorted in disgust and asked, "If they're lost, how do you know they're there at all? I play daredevil on the silver screen, Elvira. In real life, I'm too fond of my profile to risk it for what you two are paying! I've had it with this expedition. The rest of you can go fight all the wild Indians you like. I'm going back to the coast!"

There was a growl of agreement, and as Morrison bent to shove one of the canoes into the water, Wayne, Parsons, and Baldwin moved to help him.

Elvira gasped, "Stop them, Dick!" So Captain Gringo said, "Stop it, guys. You're not going to make it unless you take along some supplies. Maybe I can get a couple of porters and their mujeres to go along with you, too. Gaston's right about those coastal swamps."

The would-be deserters stared at him, bemused. Elvira jumped around like a little kid trying not to piss her britches and said with a gasp, "You can't be serious, Dick! We can't let them go! We *need* them!"

Captain Gringo shook his head and said, "No, we don't. I learned in the old Tenth Cav, the hard way, it's better to separate the men from the boys *before* you get to Apache country. When push comes to shove, I like to have only the other side to worry about. I still think the rest of you are nuts to push on now. But if you insist on marching into a mighty spooky unknown, I insist on leaving the undetermined behind. We won't get a chance as good as this one to shed excess baggage, once we leave this river bend behind."

Elvira snapped, "God damn you, Sir! My *husband* is in command, not you!"

Captain Gringo was too polite to say Professor Slade wasn't even in full control of her horny old snatch. He said flatly, "We do things my way, or I'm picking up my marbles and going home, too. You hired Gaston and me as your guides, not your executioners. If you want to push on sensibly, we'll try to keep you all alive. If you want to commit suicide, you're on your own. So what's it going to be?"

She said, "I'm not used to being spoken to that way, Young Man."

He didn't answer. He'd known that for some time. She wilted first and said, "Very well. I hope you know what you're doing."

He said, "I do." Then he turned to the would-be deserters and said, "I'm going back to the main camp. You guys wait here if you know what's good for you, and I'll send anyone else who wants out to join you. I hope you can see that the more you take along, the better your chances will be. If you cut out before sunset, shorthanded and without supplies, lots of luck. You'll need it."

He turned away and headed for their camp in the jungle without looking back. When he did, awhile later, he was mildly surprised to see that Ferris and Simpson, as well as the Slades, Dillon, and all three single girls were still with him. But he'd learned in the past that some pansies could fight pretty good. For one thing, they got more practice than the average guy who only propositioned people smaller than him.

The porters who'd tagged along as far as the grim discovery by the river looked brave or foolish, too. But when they reached the forted-up camp, and the natives who'd seen the mess had a chance to tell the others about it, there was no shortage of volunteers when Captain Gringo said there was room in the canoes for bow and stern paddlers, with their mujeres.

He chose four mestizos who looked strong as well as scared skinny, and told them to get over to the river pronto with their girl friends and such survival gear as they could all pack among them. Then he announced that nobody else was going and asked how come some idiot had built a fire with the sun going down. The camp cook asked if Captain Gringo did not wish for to eat his rice and beans hot, and Captain Gringo said, "Not with hostiles prowling as close as they could be prowling, Muchacho. Cold rations and coffee can't kill us. Arrows can."

By the time the natives assigned to get the weak sisters back to the coast had left, the sun had thumped down, and it got black as hell. One of the girls struck a match to light her tent lamp. Captain Gringo shouted across to douse that fucking light. Then, remembering his manners, he said to the nearby Slades, "Sorry. But there's no sense drinking cold coffee if we're going to light up the tents like Japanese lanterns. I sure hope it starts to rain again."

Elvira Slade said, "My God, it's so dark I can't see either of you or my hand before my face, Dick!"

He said, "That's the general idea. It's hard to aim an arrow at anything you can't see."

Slade brightened in the darkness and said, "Oh, right. We're safe from any possible attack now, right?"

Captain Gringo shook his head, even though nobody could see it, and said, "Wrong. An attack's always possible, Professor. But not too probable, if they haven't already scouted us. You folks had better go to your tent and see if you can catch some sleep. I'm going to shift some bales and boxes around our improvised fortifications. Guys tripping over things in the dark can make a lot of noise."

Elvira Slade fumbled for Captain Gringo in the dark, caught him by a very odd place, and said, "You'll have to guide us, Dick. I have no idea where I am right now!"

As a matter of fact, she was trying to get inside his fly with her naughty fingers. So he took her hand in his, and she tickled his palm all the way as he led them through the almost but not quite total darkness to their tent across the circle. He wondered what she was doing to her husband's hand as she led *him*. But he didn't ask. It was amazing how innocent the old bawd could keep her voice as she thanked him, trying to unbutton his fly again with her husband not three feet away.

He told her not to mention it, just as innocently, while he twisted her wrist in the darkness to teach her some manners. She laughed and ducked into her dark tent as Captain Gringo moved away, cursing under his breath.

He called out blindly to Gaston, who replied from somewhere nearby, and said, "Gaston, I'm going to be somewhere along the barricade for now. I'll break out the Maxim and sort of let it tag along with me. Will you make sure everyone's in the tent or shelter they're supposed to be, and tell them all to stay put unless we post them somewhere?"

Gaston said, "Oui, when one is standing guard, blind, with a machine gun, one should avoid pussy-footing up behind him, non?"

"Why do you always explain what I just said to you, Gaston?"

"My mind does not work as well when my mouth is not running. I have been thinking about that machine gun and the extra rifles. They are our property now, non?"

"I don't know who *else* is liable to claim them in the near future. So what?"

"So what if we placed a loaded Krag every few yards along the barricade, in the event of a general alarm?"

"Good thinking. As you make sure where everyone is for the night, tell them where to flop behind the arrow-proofing, when and if. I think the dames should just flatten out behind the piled gear. Tell the guys about moving at least a yard one way or the other every time they fire blind into the dark and . . ."

"Now who is telling whom how to build the clock of his grandfather?" Gaston cut in, adding, "Leave internal security to your elders, Dick. Just make sure nobody sneaks in from those adorable woods all about, hein?"

They split up. As he heard Gaston muttering and cursing at people behind him, Captain Gringo groped his way to where he hoped to find the weapons; and, finding them, hauled out the Maxim and armed it with one belt. Then he piled more nearby, as he propped the weapon over a handy crate. He found some burlap bags of beans or rice—it was hard to tell—and used them to both sandbag the Maxim in place and, piled behind it, as a soft reclining ramp to fire prone from, should he have to. He sure hoped he wouldn't. His field of fire was dark as a black cat in a coal cellar at midnight. He'd positioned the Maxim with its muzzle to the west, since that was where they *might* be coming from if they were coming. He'd considered an attack from the north, south, or east. But there was no sense trying to play chess in a world that usually played checkers, and there were only three chances out of four he was wrong.

He looked up, got his bearings by the little starlight he could see through patches in the canopy, and groped his way to the lab boys' tent. As he approached, he heard Simpson hissing, "Watch those fucking *teeth*, you silly little bastard!"

Captain Gringo coughed politely and called in, "Hey, do you guys have that moving-picture projector in there, and, more important, how does its lamp work?"

Simpson's voice sounded strained as he answered, "It's got an Edison bulb powered by a battery pack. Cut that out, Ferris. What do you want with a moving-picture projector, for God's sake, Travis?"

Captain Gringo said, "I want to use it as a spotlight. Mind if I strike a match?"

"I wish you wouldn't. We don't *have* it. I told you Pru and Sally borrowed it. Their tent's just down the line."

Captain Gringo thanked them and moved on, but not before he heard Simpson groan, "Oh yesss! Faster, faster, you fucking faggot!"

The tall American grimaced in distaste, and then, since there was no telling who was eating whom in the tent next door, stamped his feet and coughed some more before calling out to the girls inside. It had to be Pru Dorman who stuck her head out. He could see her unbound blond hair as a slightly paler shade of black. He said, "I need the projector. You can keep the film."

She told him to come in, in an innocent tone, and struck a match. He saw she was wearing a thin nightgown. He couldn't see what Sally Burnes was wearing as she stared up at him from under her bedding. Pru pointed her free hand at the projector standing on its tripod in a front corner and said,

"You'll need that power pack on the floor, too. It's terribly heavy."

Sally rolled out from under her covers. He saw she was wrapped in a heavier robe. She said, "We'd better help you. What are you going to light up with it, Dick? You and Gaston didn't do things this way the last time we camped."

He said, "We won't do them this way tomorrow night if we last that long. The idea is to set up different each time. Makes life complicated for the other side. They usually scout you before they attack and . . . Never mind. I'd better get this gear out to the machine-gun nest."

He folded the tripod legs together and put the projector across his shoulder. He'd already noticed there were no film reels attached to it tonight, dirty or otherwise. He bent to pick up the battery pack by its handle. He grunted and said, "You're right. It's heavy. Lead and acid, right?"

Pru, the expert, said, "Generator, too. You can recharge the cells by cranking that handle on the side an awful lot. I give it a couple of turns every time I think about it. Be careful of that cable running from the power pack to the projector, Dick. Are you sure we can't help?"

He grunted himself erect and said, "No, thanks. I'm not being a hero. I just don't want more than one set of feet stumbling in the dark under this load. You girls try and get some shut-eye. We're moving out at first light, fast, with no breakfast."

Sally said, "Oh, it's so much *fun* to go camping with you. But we wanted to take more shots of camp activity, Dick."

"Another time, unless you want to see more activity than I do. I keep telling people we're in Indian Country and that the Indians are on the warpath, but nobody seems to be able to hear me!"

He struggled his way back to the Maxim position without dropping anything. He heard sleepy voices behind him in the darkness, but there was nobody around to help him as he set up the projector near and above the machine gun. Then he swore at himself for not having thought to ask either girl how the damned thing worked.

But he only had to fiddle with a few switches he felt on

one side above the hand crank and, sure enough, there was suddenly a bright beam of light lancing out through the trees. It didn't flicker. Obviously that was caused by, yeah, the shutter, which opened and shut as one turned the crank. He turned the crank slowly till the light winked out, even with the bulb still burning inside. Then he switched off the bulb to save the battery power. If he heard anything out there, he only had to rise, switch on the lamp, and drop safely back down in the darkness. Then he could just reach up and move the crank handle an inch or less to have plenty of light on the subject.

He reclined on the beanbags and lit a claro. If he held it cupped below the level of the barricade, it was safe to smoke, at least. Otherwise, he faced a long, boring evening, he hoped. The only thing worse than standing guard, nine hundred and ninety nights out of a thousand, was that one night in a thousand when it mattered.

Gaston came to join him, saying, "Eh bien, there you are, my adorable firefly. Would you mind terribly if I relieved you around three, Dick?"

Captain Gringo frowned up at him and said, "I sure as hell would! It's barely eight, if that, you lazy old basser! Since when does an old soldier like you need seven hours' sleep at a stretch?"

Gaston laughed sheepishly and said, "With luck, I may get four."

"Oh? What *other* kind of luck have you been having? I sure hope you haven't been dumb enough to replace one of those missing actors in the heart of the professor's wife."

"Mais non, at the moment she seems to be in bed with that cameraman, Dillon. And I don't think he has it all the way up to her heart, despite her demands to shove it in harder. I just passed Dillon's tent in the dark, and it was très amusé. My own intended passion is called Ramona. She took one look at the leaky canoe her ex-paramour intended to float down the Verde in and returned to me, her true love. I am so hard-up I could screw her for a week if she was ugly, and Ramona's not bad-looking."

Captain Gringo laughed, but said, "Okay, but only if you make sure none of the other mestizos have her spoken for."

"Merde alors, you say *I* worry too much. The others have their own pussy bedded down with them for the night. So now, if you will excuse me, I'd better get back to mine. She says she's always admired older men."

Captain Gringo let him go, warning him he'd come looking for him if he wasn't back before three. Then it got boring as hell.

Half an hour later he heard something on the wrong side of the barricade. He rose cautiously, switched on the shuttered projector, and dropped down behind the Maxim before he reached up to open the shutter and flash a beam of Edison light in the eyes of a startled possum. He knew it would just stand there frozen till he shot it or switched off the light. Machine-gunning a possum would have been silly. So he clicked the shutter and flipped the switch off as the night creature scampered off.

He wasn't as annoyed with the false alarm as a greenhorn might have been. Night creatures didn't move around much when there were more dangerous two-legged critters in the neighborhood. The raid had probably been hit and run, after all. He'd probably never know why they'd wiped out the trading post. With luck, they'd never meet the guys who'd done it.

He heard a feminine voice call his name softly. He said, "Over here," and Meabh O'Connor joined him behind the Maxim. She was wearing the same terry-cloth robe, and it was still wide open down the front as she sank down beside him. He hauled her in for a kiss and a feel. She laughed and said, "Down, boy. I just wanted to see where you were. *Feel* where you were, anyway. Stop feeling me up. You're getting me hot."

"That was the general idea. Have you ever made love on a beanbag?"

"No, and I don't think we'd better. What if somebody comes?"

"That was the general idea, too. What did you come out here to do if you suddenly don't like coming?"

She moved his hand away from her naked lap and said, "I just wanted to find out when you're free to sleep with me in my tent, where we can do it right. I don't want to make love on the ground like a *pig*, Dear!"

He held her closer and said, "Don't knock it till you've tried it. I can't get away from here for a good six or seven hours, Doll."

She sighed and said, "Oh damn, I'll never last that long. I've been gushing for you all day. But I'd just die if someone caught us in the act!"

"We'll have to be very sneaky, then, right?"

She laughed and lay back in sweet surrender on the soft beanbags as he dropped his pants and rolled atop her. She hissed, "Oh, yesss!" as she moved her hips to meet his thrusts and pulled his shirt up to bare his chest for her naked breasts at the same time. The result was a great little quickie he'd needed more than he realized. But once she'd come and he was just getting interested in coming again, Meabh said, "Stop it. I'm too nervous about getting caught out here in the open to do it *right*! Come to my tent when you get off and—"

He cut in, "Damn it, I'm trying to get off again, Honey!" But she insisted, and he dismounted, still hard as a rock, but what the hell, once was better than nothing.

She pulled her robe together and sat up, saying, "At least now I know you'll have to be good until we can be *bad* some more."

He asked what that was supposed to mean as he wiped himself with the kerchief, still damp from having helped Sally with her soiled skirts. She said, "I saw the way those other girls have been flirting with you, you brute. Which one do you find the most attractive?"

He started buttoning his pants again as he chuckled and said, "Gee, I just can't make up my mind. Old Elvira sure has a nice shape, though."

"You goof." She laughed, kissing him on the cheek and getting up to slip away with a parting shot about expecting him by midnight if he expected to get any more that night.

He didn't argue. He was a little pissed at her, though. It hardly seemed fair to give a poor guy an erection if you weren't going to treat it right. He knew by the time Gaston relieved him they'd both be too sleepy to make love and it would serve her right. He'd learned the hard way not to wake sleeping beauties at 3:00 A.M. Maybe one in a hundred enjoyed waking up with an unexpected dong in her; the others tended to wake up spitting and scratching, and old Meabh was starting to show a touch of temper, even when she was on her best behavior.

He sat up to look around for the cigar he'd lost in all that confusion. At least it had gone out on the damp forest duff. He struck a match, saw it, and picked it up to light it again. The first couple of drags tasted like shit, but when there were no tobacco shops in the area, a knockaround guy couldn't be picky.

The match flare, short as he'd kept it, must have given his position away. Sally Burnes came right to him, flopped down on the sacking still warm from Meabh's derrière, and said, "I'm not used to going to sleep this early. I wondered if I could do anything to help you out here, Dick."

He made sure where he put the cigar down, this time, before he took her in his arms and said, "There sure is, Honey."

She kissed back warmly enough. But when they came up for air, she grabbed his wrist to remove his hand from the front of her own robe and gasped. "Are you crazy? I meant I came to see if you needed help setting up the projector, you idiot!"

He rested the hand on the curve of her trim hips as they lay side by side on the beanbags and said, "If I'd needed help with a thing like that, I'd have asked for it. Do we have to go through all this dumb porch-swing conversation, Sally? Neither one of us is sweet sixteen. Queen Victoria can't see us in the dark, even if she's looking, and, frankly, I don't like teases."

"You are a brute!" she sobbed as he pulled her closer to kiss her again. But she didn't struggle more than the invisible Queen Victoria probably required her to, and when he got his hand inside her gown again, he was pleased to discover she was built nothing like the lady he'd been making love to a few minutes ago. Her curves were smoother, but her flesh felt oddly softer than the more hour-glassed redhead's. He wondered how they differed where it really counted. But as he slid his hand down her soft, quivering belly, Sally whimpered, "Please be gentle, Darling. I've never done this sort of thing before and . . ."

"Oh shit, that does it." He sighed, stopping with his exploring fingertips just touching the fuzzy brown edges of her pubic hair as she put one of her own hands on the back of his as if to guide it, asking, "What's wrong, Dick?"

He said, "I hardly ever rape virgins, and I don't like to be accused of even trying. Like I said, we're both full-grown, and if you've been saving yourself for Mister Right since you cut your wisdom teeth, you sure must be dumb. How many innocent maidens track a guy down in the dark, in an open kimono, after they've been watching dirty moving pictures a lot?"

She gasped and asked, "Who told you we've been showing stag films in our tent, damn it?" and he said, "Me. But let's not argue about it. If you don't want me to play Chinaman to your French girl, we'll just say no more about it."

She giggled and said, "Oh, you brute, you must have *peeked*! It wasn't my idea. It was Pru who set up the projector to show those naughty films."

"Right, you'd rather have the real thing. Or do we have to go on with this charade? It's lady's choice tonight, Sally. I don't like to play kid games."

She said, "My God, I knew you were hard and bitter. Do you have much luck with such a romantic line, Dick?"

He shrugged and said, "I probably miss out on lots of stuff a guy could get by putting on an act. But I'm not an actor. I like to make love to no-nonsense, friendly dames. It's not as hard to find them as you might suppose. So do you want to fuck or don't you?"

She flinched, called him an utter bastard, and moved his hand down to rub it against her own moist clit as she sobbed, "Oh God, it's too late to stop now, even though I know I *should*!"

Then she got to work on his buttons, all of them, as he got

into position to mount her. She was still pissing and moaning about his uncouth manners when, exposed from the crotch up, he settled down against her own exposed torso in the darkness and entered her hot vagina with the erection Meabh had left him with. It served them both right.

As she felt what was getting into her, Sally gasped, "Oh God, I knew I should be afraid of you! You're a big wild animal and . . . Yesss! *Mate* with me, my tiger! I feel so wild and wicked, rutting with a brute like you out under the open sky like a bitch in heat! I don't know how I'll ever face myself in the morning, but right now I just don't care and . . . oh . . . I'm almost there, there, there! More! More! More!"

He came with her. But even as he ejaculated in her, Captain Gringo couldn't help wondering if he'd bitten off more than he could chew. She was as nice a lay as Meabh. At least he thought she was, right now. He couldn't wait to put it in the redhead again to make sure. But just how he was going to manage the two of them without an unseemly catfight was starting to concern him, now that he'd come back to his senses with another come.

But the fat was in the fire. So when Sally suggested a position she'd noticed on the silver screen and wondered about, it seemed only common courtesy to toss it to her dog-style as she moaned it made her feel like a barnyard brute and asked him if he'd ever done it this way with a real barnyard brute. He said he'd never herded sheep that long and asked if he'd missed something interesting they had on film. She arched her spine and wagged her tail with him sliding in and out of her as she laughed softly and said, "We do have a shot of a girl who seems to love her pet Great Dane an awful lot. Pru says that when a dog puts it in, he can't take it out until he's finished coming, over and over again."

"Well, the blonde may know more than me about doggy dongs. I've never had one in me."

Sally hissed, "Oh, I like what's in *me* now! Could we turn over and finish right, though? I love it when you crush me with your big brutal body!"

He liked it too, as they finished old-fashioned, with her

drumming her bare heels against his bounding buttocks—although he could have done without her nails digging into his back so sharply. He came in her again, and as she'd come twice in the meantime, asked if they could just settle down and do it some more more sedately. She sighed and said, "I'd better get back to the tent before Pru comes looking for me."

"That's all right. I don't mind if the blonde wants to join us."

Sally shoved him off to one side as she laughed and said, "Don't you dare make a pass at Pru! She'd scratch your eyes out. She's, ah, sort of lesbian, as a matter of fact."

He propped himself up on one elbow to ask, "What sort of lesbian does that make you, Sally?"

She hissed, "Don't you dare call me that! Pru is the only one who's really queer. I just have, well, *needs* I'm not perverse by *choice* like her."

He shook his head and chuckled, saying, "I stand corrected. You're not the first to point out my error. I just never knew until recently, it's not queer to make love to a queer if one's heart is pure or something."

Sally, meanwhile, had sat up and wrapped herself more sedately in her robe. She must have cooled off as quickly as she heated up. For she now sounded really pissed as she said, "Oh, I don't know why I told you that! I don't know what could have come over me tonight! I actually let you . . . *touch* me! You . . . you took advantage of my *sympathy* you mean thing! I suppose now you think I'm as low as you are!"

He didn't point out she'd actually been lower, since he'd been on top. He just asked her what the fuck she was talking about.

She gasped and said, "There you go talking dirty again! You're a dirty, dirty thing, and I don't know why I ever gave in to you and . . . yes I do. I *didn't* give in. You *raped* me!"

He snorted in disgust and said, "Gee, I'm sorry I raped you, Ma'am. But I won't tell if you won't."

She got to her feet imperiously, to say, "Don't you dare even hint to any of the others I was ever alone with you out here tonight! I'm sorry I ever came now!"

"Yeah, lots of people are sorry they came, once they've come a few times."

"Oh, you're just awful, and I never want to speak to you again!" She sobbed, turning to flounce away in the dark. He chuckled, buttoning his pants again as he wondered how serious she'd been about that last offer. He hoped she'd meant it. He was going to be in a hell of a mess if she and Meabh ever wanted some at the same time. They *both* had unpredictable tempers!

It was raining again by dawn, and everyone in camp woke up early—nervous but still alive. Two out of three wasn't bad. To keep it that way, Captain Gringo ordered cold breakfasts in shifts so they could strike camp at the same time. He tried again to talk the Slades into turning back, and when that didn't work, they struck out to the west.

The rain let up around 10:00 A.M. The day would have turned to a scorcher had they been forced to march in the open. But while the overhead canopy let just enough sunlight through to dapple the dank forest duff with little dancing dots, the misty air at ground level was almost uncomfortably cool and the greenhorns' boots were starting to turn green along the seams as well as softer on their clammy socks.

They made good time until their luck and the virgin growth gave out at noon. As Captain Gringo stared morosely at the wall of vine-laced gumbo-limbo and palmetto blocking further progress ahead, the Slades and some of the others joined him to ask what was holding up the parade. He pointed with his chin and said, "Second growth. I hope we've hit a cross trail. If that's a streak of slash-and-burn, we're going to have to work harder to mâchete through it."

Dillon, the cameraman, set up his camera, saying, "Now that's my idea of what a jungle should look like. The light's better here, too."

The blonde acting as his self-appointed assistant, Pru Dorman, asked what slash-and-burn might be. Captain Gringo said, "There's no 'might' about it. The natives gird five or ten acres of tall timber to kill and dry it. Then they burn it. Then they plant corn or cassava in the ashes. The fertility gives out after two or three crops. So they cut another clearing next door, and so forth until you can wind up with a streak of tangle like this running for miles through the virgin timber like a worm through an apple."

Professor Slade said, "That doesn't look like burned-out forest ahead, Dick. It looks like a monstrous hedgerow."

Captain Gringo sighed, and explained patiently. "After the Indian farmers move on, the weeds move in. As you can see, the competition's tough, so the second growth has to be tough, too."

He turned, waved one of the native straw bosses closer, and said, "We need some good mâchete work here, Alvorado. You pick 'em, and when they wear out, put fresh workers into that mess. You know how it's done. What are you waiting for, a pat on the head?"

Alverado laughed and went to find a couple of peones he didn't like. Captain Gringo said that, as long as they were stuck awhile, they may as well eat. Gaston suggested fires for a change. The younger soldier of fortune thought, shrugged, and said, "Okay. If there were any Indians still farming these parts, it wouldn't be so much work to get through de ol' plantation."

So, in no time at all, most of the expedition was sitting around sipping coffee while the mâchete teams took turns slashing and cursing a path through the abandoned Indian milpas. Captain Gringo could tell, once they were well out of sight in the greenery, that the second-growth belt was too wide to be an overgrown trail. He hunkered down with his back to a mossy tree trunk and a tin cup in his hand to wait it out.

Pru Dorman came over to ask if it was okay for her and Dillon to take the camera into the mess after the workers. He looked up at the blonde and said, "I wish you wouldn't. They're only cutting a single-file path, and that tripod could confuse the issue. We've got them relieving one another with the mâchetes every few minutes. It's hot, dirty work and they have enough to trip over.''

She said, ''But there's nothing to film from out here, now that they're working out of sight.''

He shrugged and said, ''Splice in a stock shot . . . Listen to me. Don't I sound like a travelogue producer?''

She laughed and said, ''You probably know as much about it as anyone. It's a new art form. Do you mind if I ask you a dumb question about your real profession?''

He nodded, and so she asked, ''Why couldn't we have just gone around? Those Indians couldn't have left this belt of abandoned farmland all the way to the North Pole, could they?''

He shook his head and said, ''No. But they could have cut a day's march either way, and, worse yet, they could still be clearing land at either end. I don't want to meet Indians I don't know right now. So our best bet is dead ahead, to the professor's lost city.''

''Do you really expect to find it, Dick?'' she asked. She didn't sound as though she did. He decided she was smarter than he'd taken her for. He liked pretty girls with brains. It was too bad she didn't like boys. She didn't look like a lesbian to him. But, since he hadn't slept with many lesbians, who was he to say?

He didn't know her well enough to ask personal questions. So he answered hers by replying, ''Ours is not to reason why. People are always tripping over ruins in these poorly mapped banana republics, even where it's not overgrown with unexplored jungle. I've seen funny stone stuff sprouting out of cultivated corn milpas. The locals aren't too interested in anything that happened before Hispanic Catholic times. I think they may be a little embarrassed by any pagan ancestors they'll admit to. I remember some pretty interesting statues down in Nicaragua— sitting right out in the open on an island in the lake. None of the local fishermen had any idea how long they'd been there or who carved them. The books say there *was* no Indian civilization that far south. You can't prove it by the Nicaraguans, one way or the other. Ask a native as black as the ace of spades about history, and he'll tell you what part of Spain his ancestors came from. Apparently they were all Christian knights who fought Moors and windmills a lot.''

She said, "Well, I hope we find *something* we can photograph. We can't go back with nothing but pictures of people walking through the woods, spliced together with stock shots of quaint natives praying for rain in a country where it seems to rain every day!''

He laughed and said, "Yeah, I can't wait to see those Hopi snake dancers in the Honduran jungle. How come you're so interested in the technical end, Pru? I thought you were an actress.''

She shrugged and said, "I am. My mother was too. But now my mother's too old to play ingénue roles and not a good enough actress to play character parts. I don't want to wind up like her.''

"I'd say you have awhile to go yet. You're still young and beautiful.''

"Thank you. Meanwhile, the clock is running and a girl has to plan ahead. This moving-picture business is in its infancy. But in the coming century, it promises to be as big as vaudeville is now. As I said, a girl has to look ahead. Once real plays are produced on film, there won't be as many jobs for actors; and the actors still working will have to be better. I think it makes as much sense to study filmmaking as it does to study acting more than I have. As I said, the clock's running.''

"Not that fast, Kid. You can't be twenty-five yet. And how can an expanding entertainment industry put even old and ugly actors out of work?''

She said, "Easy. Right now there's at least one modest theater in every county seat back home. That means thousands of little individual shows at least once a week, no?''

"Sure. Every hayseed likes to see a show when the crops are good. So what?''

"So, how many people will have hayseed tastes once they've seen real actors and actresses like John Drew or Ellen Terry play the scenes *right,* on film?''

He nodded in sudden understanding and said, "Gotcha. I saw Ellen Terry perform in New York once, and there's no comparison. She made the average bush-league actress touring the sticks look, well, bush-league. Once you film a play with real stars, expensive sets instead of canvas backdrops, and show them for the same prices where the tall corn grows—''

"Exactly," she cut in, adding, "I'll never be an actress like Ellen Terry. But there's a real shortage of people who know how to *make* moving pictures; and, even better, I won't have to worry when I lose my waistline. But I'd better get back to work."

As she turned and walked back to rejoin Dillon, he didn't see anything wrong with her waistline. He could tell she wasn't in a corset under those damp clothes, either.

He put the thought aside. He had enough dames to worry about around here. One of them came over to hunker down beside him. It was Meabh. The redhead asked, "Well, what was *that* all about?" and he said, "Camera angles. Tell me something, Red. Is Professor Slade really a professor, or is he something like a Kentucky colonel?"

She answered, "How should I know? I've never asked him to show me his diploma. I'm not even really working for him. Didn't I tell you I had a grant to come along and cover the comparative mythology?"

"You did *now*. How come you're writing his filmscript for him if you don't work for him, and while we're on the subject, how come a scientific expedition follows a *script*? At West Point they told us the scientific method was to gather your facts first and *then* figure out what you wanted to write about them."

Meabh laughed and said, "That is the way I'm keeping my own few notes. So far, I haven't met any Indians to ask about their mythology. Meanwhile a girl has to think ahead. Professor Slade says I'll get a credit line on his film when it's finally shown. What's so funny, Dick?"

He said, "Dames. You all act so weak and helpless. Yet you all plan ahead better than most male card-sharks."

"Oh, and just what was that blonde planning with you, Dick?" she asked in a suddenly suspicious tone.

He laughed and said, "I should get so lucky. Calm down, Red. I don't think I'd be man enough for the two of you."

Meabh giggled and said, "You were man enough for me this morning. But I'm still mad at you for waking me so late. Where were you all night when I really needed you?"

"Screwing other women, of course. You were asleep when I got off guard at three. I tried to roll you over, friendly. But you called me something awful in Gaelic. So I let you sleep."

She sighed and said, "That sounds like me half-asleep, alas."

He'd thought it was a pretty neat fib, too. Before he had to make up another, Alverado came over to them to announce they'd punched through to the other side of the tangle. So Captain Gringo rose, helped Meabh to her feet, and they started punching west again.

The trees opened up again on the far side, of course, and once they'd threaded all the gear through the mâchete slot, they began to make up for lost time. Dillon said he'd taken a nice shot of them all emerging from the "Green Hell," as he intended to title the episode. He said a stock shot of a prowling tiger, spliced in between shots of the real expedition crossing an old cornfield, would add drama to the story. Captain Gringo didn't tell him there were no tigers in Central America. He didn't think Dillon cared.

As the afternoon wore on, it got hot enough, even in the constant shade, to at least dry out their duds and socks. From time to time Captain Gringo took a compass bearing. So each time they took a trail break and Professor Slade asked which way his lost city was, Captain Gringo could point the way they'd been going and say, "That way, if it's there."

It didn't seem to cheer the professor much. During a late-afternoon break, as Captain Gringo came back from taking a leak out of sight in the trees, Elvira Slade cornered him against a tree and demanded, "Seriously, Dick, how far do you think we really are from those ruins?"

He said, "No more than twelve to eighteen hours, on your map. That's not saying it's there at all, of course. Where did you and your husband get your map, off an old prospector you met in a waterfront saloon?"

She said firmly, "Our sources are reliable," and he had to

take a backward step, since she was pushing her tits pretty firmly against his chest for some reason.

His back wound up against a massive tree trunk, with them both standing between its buttress roots, hidden from their waists down in case anyone was looking. He hoped nobody was, when Elvira reached for his fly again and said, "Forget about the lost city. It has to be there. And right now I'm more interested in other hidden treasures, Darling!"

He said, "For Chrissake, it's broad daylight and I only called a ten-minute break, Elvira!"

She ran her hand inside his pants, crooning, "I just want to see what I've been missing." And then, when his own damned flesh betrayed him, as most men's would with a soft feminine hand jerking them off, she sighed, "Oh, lovely! Is all that for poor little me . . . later tonight, of course?"

He was stronger than her and his own horny cock put together. So he pulled her out of his pants by the wrist and said, "Look, you know I think you're a handsome woman, Elvira. But a guy's got to have some rules, and one of mine involves the seventh commandment."

"Thou shalt not commit adultery? Who are we kidding, Dick? Don't you think I know about you and that little Irish snip?"

"Never mind about me and any other dames. Nobody else around here has a husband fixing to bust in on them any second!"

"Pooh, you're not afraid of the poor old fool, are you?"

"I sure am, Ma'am. Your husband's packing a gun, and the unwritten law gives him one hell of an edge on anyone dumb enough to mess with his wife! If I killed him I'd be a murderer. If he killed me he'd be a hero. You've no idea how odds like that can cool my ardor."

She laughed wickedly and said, "It didn't feel cool to *me*, Dick! It felt like a good eight inches, hot and trembling with desire for me!"

"Flattery will get you nowhere. Aren't you getting enough on the side from Dillon, damn it?"

"I never get enough. I'm a warm-natured woman, and if

you persist in treating me so mean, I'll . . . I'll tell my husband that you raped me!''

He laughed incredulously and said, "I was right. All you dames plan ahead more than we can keep up with. Do you think the professor would take your word against mine? Don't answer that. Dumb question.''

She said, "I'm saving a dance for you tonight, Dick. Be there.''

Then, before he had time to tell her to go fuck herself, which she'd probably take him up on if she could, he heard her husband coming their way, bleating like a sheep—or asking about his lost city again. It sounded much the same. Elvira trilled, "We were just talking about you, Huggy Bear. Dick says we're almost there. We'll talk about it some more tonight, won't we, Dick?''

He growled, "Let's move it out," and turned his back on them both to yell everyone else to their feet.

They moved on, faster than before, since Captain Gringo tended to walk faster when he was steamed. Half an hour later he saw, sickly, that he'd been thinking too hard about the fix he was in to be fully on his toes about worries ahead. He stopped in his tracks as shadows ahead detached themselves from the trees they'd been hiding behind. He called back softly, "Everyone stay put and let me do the talking. Gaston?''

"Oui, I'm covering you. But be careful anyway.''

Captain Gringo moved forward to meet the Indians ahead. They had no pants on, but were dressed in shapeless white cotton smocks; and some wore straw sombreros over their long, black braids. They weren't packing bows, long or short. They were armed with no-bullshit single-shot 12-gauge trade guns. As if he didn't have enough trouble, he heard footsteps behind him, and Meabh O'Connor caught up with him to wave gaily at the Indian who seemed to be in charge and call out, "Ciamar a tha thu an diugh?''

The Indians didn't answer.

Captain Gringo tried, "Utz-in puksiqual!" and Meabh said, "That doesn't sound at all like the Gaelic, Dear.''

He muttered, "It isn't. It's Maya. So are they, I hope.''

The leader came forward, shotgun muzzle lowered politely,

and said in perfect Spanish, "You speak Chorti strangely, Stranger. I did not understand La Señorita at all. What tribe is she from?"

Captain Gringo said, "Los Irlandeses. Sometimes *I* don't understand her, either. I am called Ricardo. The people with me have good hearts, too. We are looking for an old temple built by the Nohochacyumchacs that is said to lie ahead. If you and your people find this insulting to your Mam-ob, say so and we will go no further."

"You seek our *permission*, Señor? You are most unusual for a Spaniard."

"I am not a Spaniard. I am a gringo. That is why I must be careful about insulting people by mistake. This is your country. So it is for you to set the rules, Jefe."

The older Indian tried not to look pleased, looked pleased anyway, and translated Captain Gringo's remarks to his followers. So they looked pleased, too. One of them took the floor to point a lot at Captain Gringo as he made his own speech in their own murmuring woodpecker language. The one who spoke Spanish stared thoughtfully at Captain Gringo and then nodded as if he'd just added up some figures and was pleased with the results. He said, "We have heard of a tall, blond gringo named Ricardo who is said to be most simpatico to Indians being treated unfairly by other blancos. They call him Captain Gringo. Could you by any chance be he?"

Captain Gringo said, "If I was, it might not be wise for me to admit it just now. The people I am leading have good hearts. But they are working with a permit from your central government."

The chief nodded soberly and said, "We don't consider it *our* government, but we would not wish for to get a good person in trouble with it, Señor, ah, Ricardo." Then he brightened and said, "Bueno, we know the ruins you speak of. They are no longer important to my people, since we are now mostly Cristianos and, in God's truth, those of us who are not would no longer have time for a different god each day of the year, even if we could read the writing on the mossy old stones. Since you asked permission to enter our lands as a friend, it is only right that we treat you and your friends as friends."

"Thank you. My heart soars to learn the great Chorti-Maya are as courteous a people as I was told by others who admire them. Are the ruins far, Jefe?"

The Indian stared past him at the others, who were staring awkwardly from a more comfortable distance, and said gravely, "It is too far to reach before sundown, carrying packs, with women along to slow one down. I think it would be better if you all went with us to our nearby village. Our dwellings are humble. Our food is simple. But if you do not mind sharing them with people such as us—"

Captain Gringo cut in to say, "We would be more than honored, Jefe. But only if you will allow us to share our coffee and tobacco with you."

That seemed to strike the Indians as a hell of a good idea. So Captain Gringo turned, waved Slade and Gaston closer, and called out in English, "Jackpot! They're friendlies. They've invited us home for dinner, and, come morning, we can leave the supplies with them and take a romp over to the ruins. Offer them a little salt to put in their coffee, and we're sure to get volunteer guides as well."

Slade asked, "How do you know they can be trusted?"

So Captain Gringo said, "Jesus, Slade, that's stupid, even coming from you. Explain it to him along the way, Gaston. They're waiting. So let's move it out after them."

They did. As Captain Gringo walked at the head of the column with the chief on side and Meabh on the other, the redhead asked, "Are you really Captain Gringo, Dick?"

He looked innocent and asked, "Who's Captain Gringo, Doll Box?"

She said, "Come on, Darling. I told you I spoke *some* Spanish, and everybody knows who Captain Gringo is! Everybody who reads the papers, anyway."

"No kidding? What do the papers say?"

"It depends on which papers one reads. Some have Captain Gringo down as a sort of Robin Hood *cum* soldier of fortune. Most say he's a renegade and mad-dog killer."

"He sounds scary. What do *you* think he is, Meabh?"

"Kind of cute, when he's not messing around with other women. If I ever catch him more than messing around with anyone but me, I'll show you some mad-dog behavior indeed!"

She sounded as though she meant it.

Captain Gringo didn't have to worry about his confused sex life that night. The matter was taken out of hands by the Indians. Each obvious couple of the expedition was sort of adopted for the night by an Indian family. Creeping from tent to tent after everyone else was supposed to be asleep would have been pretty complicated in a village filled with happy night people who were curious about every move their honored guests made.

The agricultural Chorti lived in fairly substantial thatched houses with a log stockade wrapped around the whole village. Meabh's shorthand notes describing them as a matriarchal society was an oversimplification. Like many agricultural tribes in the Americas, the Chorti believed that the farmland cleared from the jungle, as well as the jungle itself that the men hunted in, naturally belonged to the men. Chorti women were expected to ask permission from the men if they so much as entered the jungle to gather firewood. On the other hand, since the women kept house, there was no argument that anything under a roof belonged to the lady of the house, and even her husband was supposed to ask her permission before he moved a pot out of his way. Since they were spending the night in the *village,* the visitors, including Meabh, tended to think Chorti men were henpecked unmercifully by the bossy Chorti women who took charge of everything the moment they arrived within the stockade.

Captain Gringo, Gaston, and perhaps some of their mestizo porters were sensitive enough to see that while the Chorti women tended to boss *them* around too, when it came to who sat where and ate what Indian food, the Indian women were shy and polite when it came to sharing rations with the expedition. They flatly refused Professor Slade's offer of coffee, salt, or other goodies until Captain Gringo explained it was up to Elvira, the natural *owner* of the food supplies, as far as Chorti women could see, to make the gracious offer. Since Elvira was a naturally bossy old broad, she took to the new customs as a duck takes to water; and in no time at all the guests and their hundred or so hosts were happily sharing Indian cooking and the expedition's coffee and condiments. When Meabh asked why on earth Indians preferred salt instead of sugar in their coffee, he said, "It could be worse. If they were Comanche, they'd put *flour* in it. Their tastes are different."

"Don't you mean *weird?*" She grimaced.

He shook his head and said, "No. Just different. Chinese think it's disgusting to grease our bread with butter. An Apache wouldn't eat a fish at gunpoint. Our porters like more pepper in their food than we do, and they'd probably agree with these Indian cousins of theirs that you have a sweet tooth. Nobody's right or wrong. The only people I find weird are the ones who insist that if they eat Mom's apple pie, everybody else eats Mom's apple pie or else."

They'd naturally been speaking freely in English as they sat side by side by a fire in front of one of the thatched houses, surrounded by the Indians that belonged there. So he was surprised, and glad they hadn't been talking dirty, when a blanket-wrapped Chorti woman who'd been seated silently across the fire from them all the while said, in almost perfect English, "The stories we have heard about you must be true, Ricardo. You are wise for such a young man. There are many older men, red and white, who kill people for not sharing their taste for la madre's pastel de manzana."

He laughed incredulously and tried, "Bei baaxi?" on her.

So she laughed back and said, "Your attempts at Maya are courteous but atrocious. I am called Akna. You may say I am what your porters call a bruja. Your word 'witch' seems needlessly cruel."

Meabh shot the older woman across the fire a thoughtful look. Then, since Akna was older, darker, and sort of moon-faced in the flickering firelight, decided to be friendly as she said, "Oh, wait until I get my notebook! I've been dying to meet a real Maya who speaks English. I'll bet you can tell me *lots* of your old folk tales, right?''

Meabh leaped up to go dig her notes out of the supplies piled across the village, near the gate. Akna sighed and said, ''I don't want to tell bedtime stories. I wish to speak with you about more important matters, Captain Gringo. Do you think she would be very angry if we went somewhere else to talk?''

He laughed and said, ''She sure would. But she's not my mother.'' Then he turned to the nearest porter and told him to tell Meabh, when she returned, that he had to go to an important meeting with the tribal elders. It could be true, for all he knew. If a witch wasn't a tribal elder, who was?

They rose, and Akna led him between two huts, down a dark lane next to the stockade, and into a slightly more imposing straw house. A rush light burned in a clay pot on a raised earthen shelf near the far wall, casting a soft illumination that was more a ruddy glow than real light. She shut the door drapes, saying, ''That's better. Nobody will bother us now.''

Then she led him to a pile of straw mats and sat him down before she cast her blanket aside. He tried not to gape. It wasn't easy. She now wore nothing but a green cotton loincloth. Her bare brown torso above it was breathtaking. He could see, now, that her plainer brown face was more weatherbeaten than old. No dame over forty could have had a perfect pair of big brown breasts like hers. The smooth, delightfully modeled belly under them was unmarred by stretch marks, too. An Indian woman older than sixteen was either a virgin or practicing birth control if she hadn't had a few kids by that late date.

Akna sat on her knees beside him on the mats and said, ''You may smoke as we talk, if you wish. Please don't get any . . . ah, chin chin ideas because I do not wear as many clothes as your people in the privacy of my own quarters. I have heard what they say about you and wicked women, Ricardo. But I am not a wicked woman.''

He reached in his jacket for a claro as he nodded and said, ''I'd better not be a wicked man, then. What did you want to talk about, Akna?''

As he lit his smoke, she said, "My people are in trouble. They do not know why. Perhaps you could tell me, Ricardo?"

He asked, "Who's giving them a hard time, the army or Don Nogales?"

She said, "Both. Our hunters and gum-gatherers have been fired on by men in uniform and wearing civilian clothing. We hope they do not know where this village is. If they find us, we shall have to fight them, of course. But we are such a small people, and the outside world is so big."

She looked as if she was about to cry. He started to put an arm around her to soothe her. Then he decided there was no place he could grab an almost-naked well-built lady in a way that would soothe either of them.

He asked, "What are you supposed to have done? Just between us, did any Chorti you know put Chorti arrows in some headless guys we stumbled over near the Rio Verde?"

She shook her head and said, "No. We heard about what happened there from some Mosquito, passing through as fast as they could move. The trading post you speak of lay in Mosquito country. They were afraid they'd be blamed by the soldados. They asked us about the same arrows. I think some bad person killed those white men with Chorti arrows to make it look as if Chorti did it."

He nodded and said, "They probably killed them with old-fashioned guns first. I don't believe you because you're pretty. I believe your people didn't do it because there's just no way a dozen armed whites, forted up in a tin house, are going to get taken out with short-bow arrows, no offense. Do you know what 'frame' means? Where did you learn to speak such good English, by the way?"

She said, "I know what it means to frame somebody for something they did not do. It is said that happened to you, back in Los Estados Unidos. I learned to speak English when I was younger, working for some Anglo people in Puerto Nogales. They exported bananas they bought from the old Don Nogales. I learned much, working as their housemaid for three years. I can read both English and Spanish."

"Good for you. But how did they manage to hire an

important bruja as a chica? Were you grabbed by slave raiders or something?''

She laughed and said, ''Oh, Ricardo, nobody can make a slave of a Chorti or any other Maya speaker. We gave up that silly notion years ago, in the days when the Yumil Qax-Ob were still said to rule the world. My position as bruja here was inherited by me from a great aunt who was still alive. We brujas live longer than the other women because we do not have children. While I was waiting to take her place, I thought it would be good to learn as much as I could about the world. A bruja who is ignorant would be of little use to her people, no?''

He chuckled and replied, ''They say Sitting Bull subscribed to the *Army Times* and Washington *Post*, too. It must have helped him foresee the future better than the average Sioux, when you think about it. Your people are lucky to have such a wise bruja, Akna.''

She shook her head sadly and said, ''I wish I *could* tell the future, now! Why has Don Nogales turned on us so? We have done nothing, nothing, and his father, the old Don Nogales, was always most simpatico. He understood us. We understood him. Neither had anything the other wanted. So we left one another alone.''

He said, ''So I've heard. What about the trader, Breslin?''

''He was not a bad person. We had more to do with him than the banana planters, of course. Señor Breslin has traded in these parts for many years. He never did anything bad to us. So we never did anything bad to him or his men. He did not mistreat the Mosquitos or Pipil, either.''

''What about Sambo?''

''There are no Sambo anywhere near here. Besides, it would be foolish for any tribe to wipe out the traders who brought nice things for them into the jungle, no?''

He grimaced, blew smoke out his nostrils, and could still smell rotten corpses as he said, ''*Somebody* must not have liked them. What do you know about the mestizos who tried and failed to stage a revolution a few days ago, Akna?''

She shrugged, which did amazing things to her big breasts, and said, ''We heard a little gossip about it. We don't really know the details. That makes no sense, either. There is hardly any government this far from the capital, anyway. What were they rebelling about?''

"I asked you first. Skip it. Let's get back to the slave-raiding and other odd habits of the new Don Nogales. He sure acts odd, for a Harvard man.''

She frowned and said, "I know nothing about him. I would not even recognize him if we met. He was only a little boy when I worked in town. Why do you say he is a slave raider, Ricardo?''

"Hasn't he been grabbing slaves to pick bananas? That's what the mestizos say. They say he hasn't been hiring his usual labor force because he's enslaved some Indians to work a little cheaper.''

She turned to stare at him soberly. She had pretty eyes, and that moon face wasn't really ugly once you got used to it. She asked, "What Indians? The Mosquito and Pipil have run away. So *they* can't pick bananas for him. *My* people, as I said, gave up slavery long ago.''

He smiled thinly and said, "I didn't know slave raiders gave the people they caught a say in the matter, Akna.''

She frowned at him as if he were retarded and said, "Of course they do, if they are real people, Ricardo. Do you know why those ruins your friends are so interested in are ruins today? In the days of the Yumil Qax-Ob, my people *were* slaves. A handful of aristocrats and a god for every day in the year made them work from dawn to dusk, day after day and lifetime after lifetime, to build stupid stone temples to their stupid gods. Then, one day, my people decided *they* were acting stupid too. So they just stopped.''

He blinked and asked, "Is *that* what really happened to the Maya empire?''

She answered, "What Maya empire? The *people* were no better off working like ants for a few foolish men with foolish notions. We *Maya* never fell. We live better today than we did when we had to waste so much time and blood for a few crazy people who told lies to us. They said if we did not do everything they told us to do, their gods would kill us all. For a long time we believed them. Yuncemil, Usukan, and the bloody Ah Puch were very frightening gods, even without the *others* to worry about. But the ruling class pushed us too far. People began to wonder what could be worse than the life they were living. So one day they just stopped. The priests raged. They threatened the people with death and misery if they did not get back to work. But the people said they were already miserable and that Ah Puch was already demanding their children's blood. So why should they go to the trouble of delivering human sacrifices if the punishment for not doing so was only death? They waited for death, meanwhile eating better and resting more than they'd ever been allowed to in their lives, but guess what happened, Ricardo?''

He laughed and said, "Don't have to. You're still here, eating the same food, living in the same grass houses, and a lot better off. I wish other people in other parts could be as smart about their self-appointed leaders. The world would be more peaceful, and when you get right down to it, who needs pyramids?''

"Nobody," she said. "You and your friends can carry them away with you when you leave, for all we care. But let's get back to *important* matters. *You* found our village, Ricardo. Do you think those *bad* men will?''

He said, "I'm not even sure who the bad guys are yet. But we'll be here awhile, and if they show up while we're in the neighborhood, they could get in big trouble.''

"We have heard you are a great fighter, Captain Gringo Ricardo. But there are so few of us, and half of us are women!''

He said, "We've enough rifles to turn some of the dames into tough-enough guys. I've got a machine gun to play with, too. Do you know what a machine gun is, Akna?''

"Of course. A machine that shoots bullets. But will you help us? *Why* should you help us? It is not your fight.''

He said, "Sure it is. We just agreed *they* were bad guys, didn't we?''

"But you said you did not know who they were. What if they turn out to be your fellow tribesmen, Ricardo?''

He smiled a little bitterly and said, "One of the only advantages of being branded a renegade is that I get to choose my friends and enemies as I and I alone see fit. I like your people. That makes your enemies my enemies, see?"

She wiped at her eyes as if she had something in them. Then she stared at him as cigar-store Indian as ever and asked, "Do you mean that? Are we really to be friends, to the death?"

He said, "Let's not talk about dying. Let's make 'em *work* at it!"

She leaned toward him, took him in her arms, and pulled him down to the mats with her, sighing, "Bueno. Chin chin is not wicked between true friends. But please do not be hurt when I tell you I can only do this with you once."

"We get to do it *once?*" He blinked, not at all confused about what "it" was as she pulled her skimpy loincloth off and out of the way. She lay submissively, brown thighs opened wide in welcome as she said simply, "My vows do not allow me to make love more than once each moon. More would weaken my powers. A bruja must be stronger than other women."

He didn't argue. He was too busy shucking his own clothes as, at the same time, he lowered his face to hers to kiss her and shut her up before she could change her mind. Some Indians didn't know how to kiss like white girls. But Akna had said she'd studied the ways of the outside world. He wondered, idly, who'd taught her to French kiss so good. But he didn't ask.

As he mounted her, Akna gasped, "Oh, what a glorious Backlum Chaam!" and he didn't need a translation. That Maya girl he'd met in Tehuantepec had admired his dong a lot too, as he recalled. He tried to decide which of them took it best as Akna took him nice indeed. Whoever had said the Maya were dying out because they had low sex drives had obviously never been in either!

Akna's moon face got prettier by the bounce as he pounded her and she pounded back. The semisolid surface formed by the thin mats on the hard-packed earth presented her tight but hungry love-maw at a lovely angle as their pubic bones ground together. He exploded in her and then, since it still felt so great, kept going. She smiled adoringly up at him in the dim red light and said, "Oh, how I wish, at times like this, we brujas did not have so many rules. If only I were a simple woman, we could make love like this all night."

"I don't get to stay the night?"

"Of course not, Dear. Once you satisfy yourself completely, you must leave."

"That part sounds like fun. But don't you mean once we're *both* satisfied?"

"Oh no, it would drain my powers if I allowed *myself* to have an orgasm."

"Akna, no offense, you're talking crazy! Damn it, Girl, I'm screwing you silly, in case you hadn't noticed. Aren't you supposed to get *anything* out of this?"

"Oh, it feels very nice. And each time you come in me, I gain some of your great strength. Do not concern yourself with me, Ricardo. *Use* me. Do everything you wish to me. I told you we were friends."

He growled, "I've heard of a kiss to seal the bargain. But this is pretty weird." And then, since if that was the way she wanted to play it, he decided to just let himself go without waiting for her.

As he did, trying to climax as quickly as he could to get out of this ridiculous situation, but naturally taking longer this time, Akna rolled her head from side to side on the mats, gasping, "Oh, not so fast! You are getting me too excited and . . . No! No! I do not wish to go all the way with you! I must be strong for my people and you are making me feel so weak and . . . oh, Bei! Bei! Baax a Kaati! You can have me, if only you will not stop! Don't stop! Don't stop! I am . . . Ayaaaaaaaaaaaah!"

He was so hot he couldn't have stopped in any case, and as he thrust hard, in and out of her climaxing flesh, she sobbed, "Not again! Not again! Is nothing sacred to you? Do you wish to rob me of *all* my power? If you don't stop this instant I shall—oh, never mind, it's too late!"

So they settled down for a good old-fashioned friendly orgy as, from time to time, she swore she'd never forgive him if she shook a rattle at something and nothing happened.

When they finally had to stop from sheer exhaustion, Akna

sighed and said, "Oh well, I never had as much power as I needed, anyway. But now my people may be in real trouble!"

He laughed, kissed her fondly, and said, "Let's hope it works like the people just quitting on the pyramids one day. Their gods didn't punish them for just enjoying life."

She said, "That was different. I'm not a made-up god. I'm a real bruja. Maybe if we stop now, I won't lose _all_ my powers."

He wasn't ready to. But then, as he lay naked atop and in her, the door drapes flew open and a younger Chorti girl popped in. She hadn't come to join the orgy. She didn't seem to notice what they were doing as she burbled at them in Maya, wide-eyed but obviously more worried about something outside than she was about catching her bruja in the act.

Akna sounded worried too, as she pushed her white lover off with a show of strength that belied all her bullshit about not wanting to climax against her will. She said, "Ricardo, if I have lost my powers it is up to you! _Do_ something!"

"Do what about what, damn it?"

"Oh, I'm sorry, I forgot how bad your Maya is. Armed men are coming this way. Many men armed with rifles. One of our scouts just came in with the news. They are not more than an hour's march away and I am so worried!"

That made two of them. So he sat up to haul on his boots, duds, and .38 to see what he could do about it.

The first thing he did was arm the people from the expedition and tell them to stay forted up behind the stockade with the Indians. The Indians had started dousing the night fires without being told, of course. As the night got darker he looked up, saw the moonlight was okay here in the clear but up for grabs out in the jungle under the dense canopy. There was nothing he could do about that. He grabbed the Maxim as Gaston grabbed a Krag and a box of extra machine-gun belts. Akna, now wearing her blanket again, naturally, told them a skinny, scared-looking boy whose name they couldn't pronounce would guide them to where he'd spotted whatever he'd spotted. He didn't speak a word of Spanish, let alone English. But the three of them headed out together anyway. A few minutes later Captain Gringo tried to remember how to say, "Slow down, God damn it!" in Maya as they staggered after the scout's dim form in the darker-by-the-minute jungle outside the village.

By the time he remembered, there was nobody in sight to yell at. Gaston growled, "Merde alors, that was a très lousy idea in the first place. We'd better stop here and set up the Maxim, Dick. Why go looking for trouble, blind, when it's coming your way in any case, hein?"

Captain Gringo said, "We have to do better than that. We're still too close to the village, and there's no way we're going to stop them all, if we can even stop any."

"Eh bien, let us go back and do it right, from behind the stockade."

"Let's not and say we did. We don't want to drive them away from the village. We want to stop them from ever *finding* it, see?"

"What is this shit of the bull about *we*? I didn't want to come to Honduras in the first place, as you may recall."

Captain Gringo plodded on, managing to just keep from stubbing his nose on a tree as he groped generally south, he hoped. They got about a quarter mile, and then he barked his shins on a fallen log and stopped, cursing.

Gaston felt ahead with his foot, kicked the log, and sighed, "Now we are not even on the species of trail, such as it was. You've managed to get us lost, you tedious child!"

Captain Gringo said, "I'm not lost. The fucking trail is. I think it's over to our left."

He was wrong. Gaston pointed off to the right and said, "Look! What can that be, torchlight?"

"It ain't fireflies," growled Captain Gringo, lowering the Maxim to the log and kneeling behind it as he quietly snicked the bolt to arm it.

Gaston dropped beside him, opening the ammo box as he muttered, "I can't believe anyone would be stupid enough to advance through Indian country waving *torches* about!"

Captain Gringo didn't answer. He was counting the flickering lights in the distance as they advanced through the trees his way. When he had it as thirty-one torches, held by at least that many stupid, brave, or probably just overconfident people, he muttered, ''Platoon-sized patrol of some kind. They look like they know where they're going.''

''Then why are they shedding so much light on the subject. Don't they think Indians are born with eyes?''

''They know thirty determined fighters armed with modern weapons are more than a match for Akna's band. The village has no more than fifty or sixty fighting men, counting the boys, and the Chorti are peasant farmers, not trained killers. Things are looking up. Those other guys don't know *we're* on the Indians' side, with our own modern weapons, and if only they don't wise up and spread out about now . . .''

He dropped lower to sight the Maxim as Gaston, who had less to occupy his mind and mouth, asked, ''Who do you think they can be, some of the mysterious Don Nogales' slave raiders?''

''Oh, I haven't had a chance to tell you. There are no slave raiders. Just assholes who wander around shooting people a lot.''

''But why? And who is working the banana crop for Don Nogales if he has neither mestizo nor Indian workers at his disposal?''

''Shut up. They're almost in range and, oh, I love it! Like ducks in a goddam shooting gallery!''

''Wait!'' gasped Gaston as they both got a better view of the oncoming targets. Save for the treacherous or frightened Mosquito Indian guiding them, every man in the column wore the uniform of the Honduran army as well as a bayonetted rifle slung on the opposite side from his torch!

Gaston said, ''We can't mow down a platoon of government troops, Dick.''

Then Captain Gringo opened up with the Maxim to mow them down indeed! The first men he dropped; of course, they dropped their torches. So the light at ground level improved as, after traversing once to blow their legs out from under the whole ragged line, he traversed the other way to blast them some more as they either flopped and barked like sea lions or just lay there. He wanted them all to do the latter. So when his gun choked dry, he snapped, "Where's that fucking belt?"

Gaston snapped the fresh belt in place, taking advantage of the lull to shout, "Idiot! Now we shall have *everybody* after us!"

"Not *those* pricks!" snarled Captain Gringo as he opened up again to finish the patrol off. The torches he'd shot them out from under were still burning all around them as he rose, drew his .38, and said, "Cover me. I'm moving in to see if I missed any."

He hadn't. Only the Indian guide and three of the uniformed men were still breathing when he kicked them experimentally. Three pistol rounds put a stop to that annoying habit.

He hunkered down to go through a few pockets. Only the one in officer's kit and a couple of noncoms had any real ID. But the money, guns, and ammo to be salvaged would come in handy. The money went into Captain Gringo's own pockets. The Indians could pick up the extra ordnance when they came to bury the dead. This close to the village, it was a good idea to plant them before they sprouted maggots.

He kicked out a few torches burning near enough to dry tinder to matter, picked one torch up, and went back to rejoin Gaston. He handed the little Frenchman the torch and said, "Here. You light the way and I'll pack the Maxim. Let's get back. All those gunshots will have worried the shit out of our people."

Gaston did as he was told. But even as he carried the torch and ammo box ahead of Captain Gringo, Krag slung, he protested, "Dick, this is crazy, even for you. Those troopers would not have been heading this way with such confidence had not they known where they were going. And if they knew where they were going, the officers who ordered them out into the jungle must have known where they were going, hein?"

"Yeah, but it answers one question that's been on my

mind. Our cutting across country worked. The fucks don't have any idea where *we* are right now.''

"Merde alors, does it matter? When that platoon fails to return, they are sure to send another and, sooner or later, they have to find us as well as the Indians!''

"Okay, so we'll have to shoot some more of the pricks. We've still got plenty of ammo. More than we were supposed to have, in case anybody ratted on us. I'm starting to wonder about that, too. Maybe they think we just got lost. Maybe they just don't *give* a shit. The professor looks like an idiot, even before he opens his mouth, and he did have a government permit.''

"Dick, if you have to mutter to yourself like that, would you mind telling me what in the seven levels of hell is going on? I'm missing something here. Who is doing what to whom, and why?''

"I'm still working on it. Once I figure it out, I guess we'll have to do something about *that,* too.''

What they did the next morning was to head for the lost ruins, with the whole Indian tribe in tow, along with all the really valuable gear they'd need in the near future. Even Professor Slade could see that, once armed whites left the Indian village, it was no safe place to raise a family.

The ruins were almost a day's march to the northwest. When they reached them, the professor looked a little disappointed. The main pyramid was impressive enough in sheer size. But it was so overgrown with strangler fig and vines it looked more like a big steep hill than a monument to anything. It wasn't three-sided, as the legends said. Captain Gringo had been wondering how one went about building a three-sided pyramid. Apparently the ancient Maya hadn't even tried. In other words, it was simply a big pile of rock surrounded by smaller rockpiles that might have been homes for the priests, cells for their sacrificial captives, ball courts, or anything else anyone wanted to say it was on the subtitles.

As the porters and most of the Indians made camp together, Dillon asked if they could clear some of the crud away so he could photograph something more interesting. Akna told some of her tribesmen to get to work with their mâchetes, and from the way they went at it, she hadn't lost all her powers after all. She still looked away every time Captain Gringo tried to catch her eye. So he quit trying. Unless he could come up with his own magic before nightfall, he was going to have his hands filled, between old Elvira, Meabh, and Sally. All three kept catching *his* eye every chance they got. The smoke signals they were sending were all too easy to read. He'd hoped at least Sally had meant what she'd said about never wanting him to touch her again. Women were so fickle-natured.

At least he didn't have to worry about the blonde, Pru. She was helping Dillon set up his cameras and, in case he changed his mind about letting her crank at least one of them, sticking so close to him a guy who didn't know better would have taken them for lovers. Captain Gringo decided that if the older cameraman made a pass at Pru, he'd kill him. Not because he wanted to wrestle with even a pretty lesbian, but for Dillon's sticking him with old Elvira! How many guys did the old bawd *need*, for Chrissake?

She told him, during their noonday dinner, when she managed to corner him alone a minute. She said her husband was usually sound asleep by nine or ten. When he said he'd promised to stand guard until midnight, she said she'd wait in his tent.

One of the nice things about the Indians they'd picked up was that, not being Hispanic, they'd never gotten into the habit of taking a siesta from noon to three or four, even when it wasn't hot. The afternoon sky was overcast and the trades had picked up nicely again. So while Dillon bitched about the lighting not being to his liking, work on the pyramid went smoothly and, as the long-covered barbaric carvings emerged from the shrubbery, a little the worse for wear, Dillon cheered up considerably and even let Pru take some shots of Indians exposing ugly faces, snakes, and what looked like either guts or decorative designs to view.

Captain Gringo climbed to the top, where some trees still grew, and sat on a god's head to smoke and enjoy, or watch, the view. It was hard to tell, from up here, whether anything was moving under the forest canopy now spread out before him below eye level, endlessly, like a fuzzy big green rug. But at least he was alone up here, and a guy had to be alone to think when there were so many disconnected things to think about.

It didn't work. Nobody bothered him for hours. But, as always when a guy faced the coming darkness with dismay, the damn day passed full steam ahead, with the hours getting away from him like minutes. It felt as if he'd barcly settled down up there before some maniac rang the supper bell. He glanced to the west and, sure enough, the crazy sun was dropping like a rock over that way.

The evening meal went down like a speeded-up comedy on film, too. His mother had always told him to chew all his food thoroughly, and that night Captain Gringo tried his best to obey. But it seemed he'd just sat down when his plate was empty and everyone else was getting up. So he had to get up too. It was darker now. So he grabbed a Krag and headed out to stand guard before anyone could stop him.

It didn't work. The redhead, Meabh, caught up with him before he could hide behind a tree and said, "Dick, we're going to have a problem tonight."

He didn't ask what was wrong. He was sure she'd tell him. She did. She said, "I don't know how to tell you this, Darling. I hope you won't get mad. But I seem to be having my period early this month."

He laughed with sick relief and said, "Better early than late. Why should I be mad. Did you do it on purpose?"

She sighed and said, "Oh, I was hoping you'd be so understanding. I can always, you know, take care of your needs another way."

He said, "That wouldn't be fair to you, Doll. I'm on guard until midnight, anyway. It won't kill me to miss a few nights."

She frowned thoughtfully and said, "We missed *last* night,

too! Where were you? I mean, after you shot those slave raiders or whatever?''

''I cannot tell a lie. I was shacked up with an Indian. For Chrissake, Red, it was almost dawn before we got that mess back there cleaned up.''

''I wouldn't have minded if you'd woke me for a quickie. Now I can't go all the way with you for at least three or four nights. But my offer's still good if you'd like some you-know.''

She licked her lips suggestively in case he hadn't guessed what she had in mind. He said, ''We'll talk about it later. You'd better get under your netting. Unless that was a woodpecker I just felt on the back of my neck, we're camped in buggy country tonight.''

She told him where *she'd* like to bite him, laughed, and scampered back to camp. He laughed too, and moved on. He hadn't really been bitten by a mosquito, but one down and two to go was some improvement. He wondered if old Elvira still had periods. He wondered if it would slow her down if she did. Old Elvira was obviously more crazy than passionate. He knew why she wanted him. It wasn't flattering to him. There were any number of guys in camp who'd go to bed with the cheating bitch and she knew it. So they didn't stand a chance with her. She only wanted guys who didn't want her. Obviously Dillon needed the job. Otherwise, an old pro like Dillon never would have made a pass at the wife of his boss. Ergo, she'd been screwing Dillon silly. Now she'd discovered a guy who liked her even less, and had to prove a point. He wondered if she even enjoyed it. He wondered why he should be wondering how she made love, even if she did have great legs. But what the hell, when rape was inevitable . . .

It never happened. It was starting to look like he had no way of getting out of it that wouldn't cause more trouble than just banging the old bawd. But after an amazingly short five hours on guard, with midnight galloping up behind him with the bit between its teeth, Captain Gringo heard two pistol shots, lots of screams, and ran toward the sounds as he snicked the safety off his Krag.

The camp was a swirling chaos as he tore into it, adding to

the general panic. Indians and mestizos were running around in every direction like chickens with their heads cut off. He spotted the blonde, Pru, staring blankly from the fly of her tent in her nightgown, and asked her what had happened. She gasped, "I don't know, Dick. It sounded like shots."

That was a big help. A barefoot Chorti woman ran through the night fire in front of him, screaming in panic or perhaps because her feet hurt. On the far side he saw Professor Slade staggering numbly toward him, bareheaded with a pistol hanging down at his side.

Captain Gringo called out, "Are you okay, Slade?" and the older man raised the gun in his hand to his face, put the muzzle in his mouth like a licorice whip, and as Captain Gringo shouted "No!" pulled the trigger.

The horror-struck soldier of fortune saw he'd been wrong about the professor having no brains, when the top of Slade's head exploded in a cloud of pink froth, gray matter, and hairy skull fragments. Then the body went over backward to land with a limp, lifeless thud. Both Pru and Sally dashed out of the tent they shared at the sound of the latest mystery shot, saw what had happened, and screamed in unison. That brought the redhead, Meabh, running, and she screamed pretty good too.

Captain Gringo shouted, "Would you all shut up and let me figure out what the hell's going *on* around here?"

He stepped around the fire to stare morosely down at the dead man, who was in no position to tell him anything. Gaston came over to them, looking a little green around the gills despite the orange firelight, and murmured, "Eh bien, so much for this one, too."

"*This* one? There's more?"

"Oui, in Dillon's tent. Très grotesque."

He followed the Frenchman to the cameraman's tent, where the lab boys, Ferris and Simpson, were looking pretty green too. Captain Gringo ducked inside. The hanging lamp was brightly burning, unfortunately. Dillon lay stark naked, as well as dead, across his bedroll. His eyes were open. His mouth wore a puzzled smile, as if he wondered who'd shot him in the chest and cut his cock off. Elvira lay on her back nearby, just as naked. He'd been right about her having great legs. Her tits were a little messy. She'd been shot from behind, so some of her heart had been blown out the gaping hole between her breasts. Blood ran from between her clenched teeth. It wasn't her blood. When the bullet had hit her spine, she'd bitten Dillon's penis off at the roots.

Captain Gringo muttered, "Jee-zuss!" and Gaston said, "Oui, a très mundane domestique tragedy, non? It is bad enough to walk in on one's wife and another man when they are simply making la zig zig. Catching her down on M'sieur Dillon must have unhinged the late professor a bit, non?"

"Unhinged a bit, my ass. The poor guy went just plain gaga! I wish he hadn't killed himself, though."

"Oui, how shall he ever pay us now?"

"That's not what I meant. I had other questions I wanted to ask him. Couple came to me just awhile ago as I was stalling for time out on guard and, Jesus, you'll never know how glad I am this bitch couldn't wait!"

Simpson had only been following the parts that were important to him. So he said, "Jesus, that's right! With both Slade and his wife gone, the expedition's a bust and we're never going to get *paid!*"

The more effeminate Ferris sobbed, "Oh God, we're broke and stranded in the jungle!"

Captain Gringo growled, "Don't you start screaming too, for God's sake. We're not stuck on a desert island.. We've got just as much to work with as we ever had, and Gaston and me know the way back."

Gaston said, dryly, "Oui, avec a très amusing and no doubt highly pissed-off Honduran army anxiously awaiting our return with bated breath!"

Captain Gringo ignored him and went down the line to where Pru and Sally were supposed to be bedded down but were actually hugging each other like frightened kids—or were they *more* than friends?

He explained the situation to them, leaving out the gorier details, and said, "You wanted to be a motion-picture producer, Pru. Here's your big chance. We've still got all the equipment and the lab boys to develop the film as you shoot it. You've got another day to shoot everything here. I think I can get the Indians to dance around for you. Then we'd better head back for the coast, pronto. I've been looking at the map. There's an easier way to get back than we took coming out. Can you do it?''

Sally asked, ''But who's going to pay us?'' And Pru said, ''Don't be a ninny! If we bring back anything worth showing, we can *sell* it!''

''But, Pru, it's not our film and equipment!''

''Of course it is. Who *else* owns it now, the *Indians?*''

Captain Gringo laughed, told her he foresaw a great film career for her, and left. He had to go through the whole story over again with Meabh in her tent. But she agreed it was a good idea and said she'd work with the other girls on finishing some sort of travelogue. She thought it might be swell to have a real white goddess posing with the Indians. So maybe there had been some point in bringing Sally along, after all. Up until now, she'd only been good for nice but needlessly complicated screwing.

He went to his own tent, leaving the guard duty to Gaston. As he got under the bedding, he had an erection. It figured, now that he didn't have to worry about getting the damn-fool thing up.

The following day was sort of interesting. Once the Indians got over laughing, they thought it might be fun to play their ancestors. So Sally got herself rigged out in as scanty a semi-Maya outfit as Akna and Queen Victoria might approve between them. Then the Indians carried Sally around while Pru cranked away at them. Meabh had appointed herself director, and the limp-wristed lab boys weren't at all interested in peeking in other tents so long as they could be alone together. So Captain Gringo managed to rob Akna's power some more while nobody was looking. He didn't just do it for fun. Aside from saying good-bye to a friend properly, he wanted to give her some instructions on the power of staying alive until he could get the people pestering her people off their backs. She said it would be easy enough to hide out the few days he promised she'd only need. So he showed her how easy it was to come, dog-style, and she said she'd never forgive or forget him for leaving her in such a powerless position.

They stayed camped where they were the following night, the Indians having buried their dead for them before fading away into the jungle like shadows.

In the morning, Meabh praised him for being so understanding and brave about toughing it through without sex, poor baby. So he didn't tell her about Sally sneaking over for a quickie during the night. Sally naturally went on looking mad at him when she wasn't begging him to come at least once more before she never spoke to him again.

After breakfast he called the survivors together, explained they were leaving everything but the gear they really needed behind, and added that he knew a shortcut back to Puerto Nogales. Nobody argued that point. The porters had been good sports about the way the professor had suddenly stopped paying them their modest day wages at the end of each day. But they saw no point in hanging around out here for free.

So Captain Gringo took the point, led them cross-country until they cut a trail, then led them east along it. They made good time. The route he'd chosen was a firm wagon trace. Toward evening, they started passing banana plantings. The bananas worried Gaston more than the others. He caught up with Captain Gringo to ask, "Dick, are you leading us where I hope even you would not be mad enough to lead us?"

Captain Gringo said, "This road leads straight into Puerto Nogales, by way of the Nogales plantation. Why?"

"Why? Merde alors, since we got here we've heard nothing but tales of what an ogre this Don Nogales is supposed to be!"

"Yeah, and we've met wild Indians who weren't wild, slave raiders who don't take slaves, and who knows what we'll find down the road ahead?"

"God damn both our mothers, you species of lamb to the slaughter, *some*body has been killing people around here!

First the rebels, then the traders, and, merde alors, now *us*, if you don't know what you're doing!''

"I know what I'm doing," said Captain Gringo, pointing at a banana stalk leaning out over the trail as he added: "Look at that. The hand of fruit is way too ripe for picking now. I think this whole crop will be lost, don't you?''

"Sacre bleu, who cares? We are not in the banana business, Dick.''

"Right. So who *is*? Hasn't it struck you odd that the only powerful interests in these parts haven't been paying any attention to the only business around here?''

"Ah, except monkey business, of course. But what is our mysterious Don Nogales up to with the monkeys, since he has obviously no interest in bananas this season?''

"Don't know, exactly. Could work more than one way. That's why we have to pay a call on the guy.''

"Just like that? Welcome to my parlor, said the spider to us idiotic flies?''

"I don't think he wants trouble with us. In the first place, why should he? In the second, if Nogales was worried about us, he'd have made a move against us by now. But, so far, he never has. He's got us down as a pack of crazy gringos, which we are in a way.''

"Ah, oui, that is why he wiped out the people we were supposed to run the guns to, hein?''

"He didn't know that. The deal between the American, Hardiman, and his confederate, trader Breslin, was something none of the locals knew about. I'm still working on the guys at the trading post. Cut a guy's head off and bake him in tin for a while and he could be anyone. Have you ever seen an isolated jungle trading post with that many clerks on duty, Gaston?''

"Mais non, now that I think about it. But what does this all *mean*, my mysterious traveler?''

"Tell you more after we travel some more. Pick 'em up and lay 'em down. I want to make the main plantation compound just after sundown.''

They did. It was about seven when they were challenged on the road and identified themselves to the gate guards at

Don Nogales' plantation. The guards said they'd heard about the expedition, didn't want to check their government permits since neither of them could read, and suggested they camp by an irrigation canal a few miles down the road. Captain Gringo explained they were tired of sleeping in tents, had always been dying for a guided tour of a banana plantation, and asked if they'd ask Don Nogales if he was receiving visitors at this hour.

Half an hour later, it turned out he was. So they followed the house servant he'd sent for them up to the main house a quarter mile off the road, where the whites in the party, at least, were graciously received on the front veranda of the imposing main house by a pleasantly nondescript youth who admitted to being Provisional Governor Don Hernan Nogales y Carzon and told them his casa was their casa. He said the pobrecitos could bed down in the bushes out back, downwind. When Captain Gringo said they had valuable gear and, of course, the clothes they'd need to change to for dinner to worry about, Don Nogales unbent enough to let Alverado and some of the cleaner-looking guys bring the stuff in.

In the better light inside, they saw the fort-like main house was built Spanish New Orleans style around a patio with steamboat verandas and balconies both wrapped around the outside and facing the insides. Nogales left them in the care of his house servants, who led them and their porters to second-story guest rooms. As soon as they were alone, Captain Gringo took Alverado aside and told him to ring the outside camp with a barricade, arm the men, and make sure nobody got in or out that night without his permission. When Alverado looked worried as well as surprised, Captain Gringo said, "I don't know these people, either. I wouldn't have led you here if I expected them to jump us. But I could be wrong. We'll know before morning."

Alverado said he understood, which was a lie, and left to carry out the strange orders. Captain Gringo went to the room the three girls had been assigned to, knocked, and went in. He gathered Meabh, Pru, and Sally away from the door and said, "We don't have time for explanations. So listen tight. Hopefully we're in for dinner at eight, dragging on until nobody can swallow another bite. Then the men and women will split up. I want you three to put on your best dresses and wear your pistols under your skirts. You may not have to use them. Hispanic ladies are not expected to fight. So the dames here may not know how.''

Sally gasped, ''Good God, Dick, what have you gotten us into?''

So he said, ''I hope we've nothing to worry about but a heavy meal and a good night's sleep before we march on to Puerto Nogales in the morning. I'd tell you more, but we haven't much time, and the less you know at dinner the less you can give away by accident.''

The blonde, Pru, didn't ask. She said, ''There's more to this Nogales family than meets the eye, right?''

And he said, ''I always thought you looked smart. If *they're* smart, they won't do anything but extend us the hospitality dumb innocents like us would expect and then send us on our way with a sigh of relief. So heads up, guns on, and we'll play it by ear. I've got to alert the pansies now.''

He did. Ferris looked more frightened than all three girls put together. But Simpson said they'd pack their guns under their dinner jackets and follow his lead. So Captain Gringo joined Gaston in the room they'd been assigned, and would have given him the same instructions if Gaston hadn't told him to make sure he wore his shoulder rig to table, adding there was something très fishy about this setup.

The Nogales house didn't look fishy. It was luxuriously appointed with its own electric plant, Edison lighting, and a telephone extension in every room. Captain Gringo swiftly changed his shirt, put on the linen jacket he'd packed away, and while there was still time, picked up the phone. He waited until the line clicked a few times and a fuzzy-voiced female operator came on. Then he asked if she was well and if she could by any chance connect him with the U.S. Consulate in Puerto Nogales.

As he waited, Gaston murmured, ''You know, of course, someone has to be listening in?''

Captain Gringo nodded and said, ''I sure hope so,'' as he

heard the other end ringing. A sleepy voice finally answered and said the resident consul had left for the day. Captain Gringo had been counting on that. But he made himself sound upset, anyway, as he said, "Take this down, then. This is Travis. Your boss will remember me as the guide assigned to the Slade expedition. Everything that could go wrong went wrong, and both Professor Slade and his wife are dead. I'm bringing the survivors in, and I'll give you a full report when we get there . . . before noon, I hope. We're spending the night at the Nogales plantation, and you've no idea how good it feels to get back to civilization after all we've been through!"

The clerk at the other end said they'd be expecting them, and they both hung up. Gaston stared at Captain Gringo fondly and said, "Mon Dieu, you shit the bull très formidable. Your balls are not bad, either, for a youth whose adorable face is probably très familiar to the consul you just failed by minutes to contact. I'm sure he has the reward poster *somewhere* in his desk, hein?"

Captain Gringo lit a cigar. He didn't get to finish it before a footman knocked on their door to announce dinner was served. As they followed him downstairs, Gaston kept chuckling to himself. Captain Gringo didn't ask why. If he hadn't wanted to reassure the people here they were just what they seemed, he wouldn't have made that otherwise pointless call for them to listen in on.

Dinner was served indeed. People in Latin America could be divided into those who had too little to eat and those who had too much to get down in less than seven courses. The handsome and courteous Don Nogales sat at one end of the table. A surprisingly young and attractive Doña Nogales sat at the other end. It was soon established she was neither wife nor mother to their host. She was his stepmother, the young widow of his late father. Captain Gringo had been seated near the head of the table, to their host's right. The uniformed older man across from him was introduced as Major Montez, commander of the modest local military garrison. There were enough other uniforms seated farther down the table to account for a pretty big officer's staff for less than a battalion.

But banana-republic armies were like that. Any younger son too dumb to be a priest usually wound up a military officer down here.

Captain Gringo was more interested in the other American directly across the table from him. Don Nogales introduced him as Señor Breslin, the well-known Indian trader.

Captain Gringo said, "I'm glad to see you're still alive, Breslin," and the other American grimaced and replied, "So am I. You heard about the Indians wiping out almost all my outposts, eh?"

Captain Gringo nodded and said, "We stumbled over one, heading out. I don't think we should talk about it at the dinner table. But we took some pictures, if you'd like to see them later."

Don Nogales poured more wine into Captain Gringo's glass as he asked if they had other pictures, adding, "The major says he's missing some of his own men in the jungle to the west. They were on a punitive expedition against the Chorti and have not been heard from since."

Captain Gringo knew neither the girls nor lab boys had come out from the village to view the shot-up patrol. So it was safe to say, "That's odd. We spent a few days with Chorti, and as you see, they didn't scalp us. As a matter of fact, we took moving pictures of them, and they were very helpful when Professor Slade went crazy and killed his wife and himself. Is there someplace we can set up a screen and the projector, later? You señores may be interested in our motion pictures."

He leaned closer to his host as he confided, "Some of them are sort of naughty."

Don Nogales chuckled and said, "No problem. After dinner the ladies will of course be leaving us to enjoy our port and cigars, no?"

The American across from him grinned and asked, "Are we talking about, ah, French movies, Travis?" and Captain Gringo winked and said, "One of the, ah, actors, looks like a well-hung Chinaman."

Don Nogales had seen the wonders of modern science, he said, during his four years at Harvard. He seemed to eat a little faster now, for some reason. So the meal went quicker than usual in Hispanic circles, even though it still lasted long enough for North Americans to have eaten three.

Doña Nogales saw something was up. So she graciously rose from her place to lead the other ladies to her salon for girl talk. Save for the three American girls, there'd been only two other female guests invited to her stepson's masculine get-together of the local power structure. Captain Gringo said he, Gaston, and the lab boys would set up the travelogue and dirty movies. As he rose, Don Nogales said the butler would show them to the biggest room in the house. He didn't offer to help, himself. Captain Gringo had been hoping he wouldn't. So, as the self-indulgent young planter dawdled over brandy and cigars with the guests that were really important to him, Captain Gringo and his helpers got to work.

The setup was even better than Captain Gringo had hoped. He'd been playing by ear up to now, but when the butler showed them to what he called a library, they saw it was a library indeed. The ceiling was two stories up, with an electric chandelier hanging to the level of the balcony running around the book-lined walls. The butler showed them where the light switch was. Captain Gringo thanked him, dismissed him, and led the others as they hauled all the stuff he needed in from where the expedition gear was piled on the patio outside. He told the lab boys to set up the projector on the balcony at one end, adding, "We'll run the dirty reel for them first. They know more than we do about what's going on in the countryside around here, and we don't want to risk the travelogue film, anyway." Then he nudged Gaston, and they hauled their own load along the balcony to the far end. As Gaston started catching on, he chortled, "I love it. All four of us will be up *here*, with them down *there*, when you decide to end this charade, hein?"

"Don't talk so much. Help me get this fucking screen set up."

They did, suspending the top of the screen from the fancy ironwork near the ceiling and letting it unroll to hang just below the edge of the balcony they were on. Captain Gringo said, "Go tell 'em the show is about to begin, while I make a few more adjustments."

Gaston did. So a few minutes later, Don Nogales and his other male guests filed in. There were only enough chairs to seat the young hidalgo, the trader, the major, and a couple of other senior officers, since rank had its privileges.

The dozen-odd lesser beings were good sports about sitting on the luxurious oriental rug between their superiors and the silver screen, which was sort of mildewed muslin when you looked closely.

As they waited with anticipation, Captain Gringo told Gaston to go up and help Ferris and Simpson while he got the lights. Then he flicked the switch by the door, and for an uneasy, muttering moment the room was plunged in utter darkness.

But before anyone could say he was afraid of the dark, the battery powered projector shot a series of numbers over their heads at the screen across the cavernous room. Then they all gaped in wonder, or giggled, as a seductive-looking lady wearing nothing but black silk stockings smiled down at them knowingly and pointed at her pubic apron as if they might not know what it was.

Don Nogales laughed in the flickering darkness and called out, "Is this your idea of a *travelogue*, Señor Travis?"

So Captain Gringo laughed sheepishly and called back, "Wrong reel. Want me to change it?" as he mounted the winding metal steps to the balcony. The planter laughed again and said, "Don't you dare! Not until we see what she does *next*, anyway!"

What the blown-up image on the screen did next was move back to a sofa and sit down, raising both knees, with French heels hooked into the sofa cushion as the silvery thighs parted to give them a better look at the biggest vaginal opening any of them had ever seen. They were most impressed, even before the actress, whore, or whatever she was, smiled sweetly down at them, wet a finger coyly with her simpering mouth, and proceeded to stimulate her own clit as, below it, her gates of love opened and closed teasingly, with astounding

muscular control. One of the junior officers shouted, "Oh
Señorita, are there any more at home like you?"

It was the last question he'd ever ask. Because, by then,
Captain Gringo had made it around to the far side of the
screen, whipped the tarp off the Maxim and, since he knew
where they'd be staring as one, shoved the muzzle of the
machine gun into the image of the pulsing snatch on his side
of the screen and pulled the trigger, full automatic.

Gaston and the lab boys got to see it all as the blown-up
black and white image of the naughty lady seemed to be
pissing fire from her love box down into the audience below.
Even machine gun bullets couldn't be everywhere at once, so
at least one poor slob made it to the door. But when he tried
to open it, he discovered Captain Gringo, thinking ahead, had
locked it. Then a machine gun slug found him and that was
that.

Captain Gringo hosed back and forth a few more times for
luck, then shouted, "Aim the beam *down,* for Chrissake!"
So, when Simpson failed to move, Gaston grabbed the
projector and swung the flickering beam down. He went on
cranking to keep from burning the film. The view was surreal
as the inflated whore's distorted masturbation continued,
superimposed on sprawled bodies, blood, and guts that weren't
doing a thing for the oriental carpeting.

Captain Gringo shoved a fresh belt into the Maxim, picked
it up, and headed for the spiral steps to ground level, calling
out as he descended them, "Mop up here, and don't run up
behind me without letting me hear your voice a lot. I gotta
see if the girls are okay!"

They were. After he'd switched on the lights in the library,
kicked the door off its hinges, and dashed outside, he spotted
the redhead, Meabh, in a doorway across the patio. He ran
across to her. He pushed on into the room the ladies had
retired to. The blonde, Pru, was standing in the middle with a
man-size revolver in her dainty hand. It was still smoking. At
her feet lay Doña Nogales, the other female guests, and,
sprawled like a broken doll in one corner, Sally.

Sally wasn't as pretty with half her face blown off. Captain Gringo gagged and asked Pru if she'd done that. The

blonde kicked the body of the fallen Doña Nogales and said, "She had a gun under *her* skirts, too. She pulled it when we heard all those other gunshots. I didn't know whose side she was on until she shot poor Sally. After that, I just kept shooting at anybody I didn't know until this stupid gun was empty!"

He nodded and said, "You did right. Reload." Then he turned to the redhead, still frozen in the doorway, and said, "You, too, Meabh, if you got any shots of your own off. I've got to see about the servant problem."

The redhead just stared through him, glassy-eyed. Some people were like that when the chips were down. He turned back to the blonde and said, "Pru, get Meabh up to your room. Lock the door and don't let anyone in you don't know until further notice."

He left them to work it out. Back out in the patio, he spotted Gaston frog-marching a bunch of the hired help at gunpoint; he hefted the Maxim to his own shoulder, saying, "Good thinking. Is that the whole staff?"

Gaston said, "It had better be. I told this species of a lying butler what would happen to him if we found any upstairs maids in the root cellar."

The butler gasped, "In the name of God, Señor Ladrone, we are neither liars nor fighters! Spare us and we can show you where the owners keep their jewelry and plate!"

Captain Gringo smiled thinly and said, "We are not bandits. We were sent here by your own central government to find out what was going on, and what we found was a mess that really needed cleaning up. We're going to turn you loose. The place will be crowded enough in a minute. But first tell me where this plantation's telephone switchboard is."

The butler looked confused and said, "When the owners wish for to make telephone calls, they simply pick up the nearest one and a lady in town does the rest, Señor. Forgive me, I know little of such matters. We servants were forbidden for to use the telephones and—"

"Better than I hoped," Captain Gringo cut in, turning to Gaston to add, "Run them off the property. Then get our own people in here on the double. We may have a siege before I can get some real Honduran troops here to police up the area.''

Gaston said, ''Oui, if they don't wind up putting *us* against the wall as well! I agree the one calling himself 'Breslin' had to be a fake if he did not know about the deal with us his own partner, Hardiman, made. But if even one of those officers you spattered across the library rug was the real thing—''

''Get moving!'' snapped Captain Gringo, adding: ''I'm setting up with this Maxim in the second-story room overlooking the main entrance. Get our own people in and post a couple of good riflemen to cover the other three sides. We can argue about how I separated the sheep from the goats after we make sure we nailed all the leaders!''

He turned away, found a stairway, and carried the machine gun to an even nicer than average bedroom on the second story. He braced the Maxim on the windowsill, straightened the ammo belt, and saw he had a nice field of fire—should anyone be dumb enough to ask for a rematch. He didn't think any survivors of a pretty slick gang would, now that the charade was over. But it was better to play it safe than wind up sorry.

He picked up the French phone by what had to be the late Doña Nogales' satin-sheeted four-poster, and when the operator he'd spoken to before picked up at the other end, he agreed it was a lovely evening, said he was sorry her mother was sick, told her his family was fine, by the grace of God, and asked her to connect him with a number in Tegucigalpa and reverse the charges por favor. It only took her a million years and two wrong numbers before a male voice at the other end said, ''Colonel Badillo, Military Intelligence. In what way may I be of service to you?''

Captain Gringo said, ''For openers, you'd better call the garrison at Puerto Cortés and get us some military police here on the double, Sir! The suspicious hanky-panky you sent us to infiltrate turned out to be a real can of worms, and at the moment, you don't have a single Honduran official above the rank of postman or telephone operator here in Puerto Nogales!''

The colonel gasped. ''Is that you, Señor Walker? We'd given you up for dead; and, as a matter of fact, a detachment of our troops should be there within the next twenty-four hours!''

"You still owe Gaston and me for nipping a really nasty situation in the bud," said Captain Gringo, adding: "Your guys would have walked into another massacre like lambs to the slaughter. Until a few minutes ago, what was passing for your military government here was the mysterious group of sudden strangers you sent Gaston and me to infiltrate! They'd heard about infiltration, too, so it was over before we got here. Then we got detoured a few days and . . . Never mind the details right now, Sir. I'll put it all in the written report you'll get when *we* get our *checks!* Right now I have to make sure we're all alive when your guys get here. We're forted up in the Nogales plantation, just out of town, and—"

"Are young Don Nogales and his beautiful stepmother safe as well?" the Honduran officer cut in. Captain Gringo had hoped he wouldn't ask dumb questions like that. He told Badillo, "The old Don Nogales died a few months ago, as you know. Probably from something he ate. There's no good guys here but us chickens; and if I don't hang up, *we* may wind up dead, too!"

Suiting deeds to his words, he hung up the phone, checked the front lawn again, and lit a smoke. He heard movement behind him and turned to see Pru Dorman standing there. The blonde said, "I gave Meabh a sedative and put her to bed. She wasn't feeling well, even before the world went insane around her. I just met Gaston outside, and he said to tell you we're well buttoned up, whatever that means."

He smiled at her and said, "It means we're in good shape to stand off any bad guys we missed, even though they're probably running like hell about now. We're behind stout walls with plenty of food, water, and ammo. About this time tomorrow, the Honduran government will be back in charge again here. I was just talking to the guy we were working for, and—"

"Dick," she cut in, "I know *some* of what's been going on has to make sense. But that's just crazy! You and Gaston *are* soldiers of fortune wanted by the law, aren't you?"

He sighed and said, "People sure do gossip a lot behind

my back these days. We are soldiers of fortune. We are wanted by the law in lots of places. But awhile back, we served in the Honduran Army, saved Honduras from a coup by rebel officers, and the winning side still remembers us with respect for our professional skills, if not with gratitude. When the head of their intelligence heard something that smelled like a revolt was brewing here, he cabled Gaston and me a money order as well as some hasty instructions. The rest is history.''

She shook her head and said, ''Not to *me* it isn't! I've no idea what on earth's been going on, and I'm still upset about poor Sally—even if she was a bit silly at times—and if you don't explain why *you've* been acting so strange, I'll never get a wink of sleep tonight!''

She sat herself on the four-poster and added, ''Now, for heaven's sake, start at the beginning and tell me the whole story, Dick!''

It was too long a tale to tell standing up. There was no other place to sit. So he snuffed out the smoke he'd just lit and sat down beside her. She didn't flinch away as the sag of the unexpectedly soft mattress put their hips closer together than he'd intended.

But even if Pru hadn't been on record as a lady who liked boys more than other ladies, bedtime stories usually came first. So he said, ''Once upon a time there was a sleepy little banana port, remote from the central government and run by a small local power structure. The few important people were all white, only socialized with one another, and of course looked pretty much alike to the few Indians and mestizos they bothered to talk to.''

Pru said, ''You mean the officers of a tiny garrison, the Creoles here at the only plantation in the area, and of course Mister Breslin, the Indian trader.''

It had been a statement rather than a question. But he answered it anyway, saying, ''Maybe a few others, like the key port officials; but, yeah, all in all fewer than five hundred people.''

They were still seated awkwardly for comfortable conversation, so Captain Gringo placed an experimental palm on the smooth silk bedding with his arm braced behind the blonde's primly positioned spine. She leaned back against it and said, "Thanks. What happens next?"

He figured she probably meant the rest of his bedtime story. So he said, "Okay, into this sleepy little Garden of Eden comes the serpent, or in this case a cuckoo bird. You know, of course, how a cuckoo sneaks her own chicks into other bird's nests when they're not looking?"

"Are we talking about that bitch who shot poor Sally?"

"We are. She was young, beautiful, ambitious, and as you saw, murderous. She married old Don Nogales, a recent widower, while his only son and heir was away at college. The old planter was too decent or maybe just too lazy to expand his banana business into the empire she envisioned, and he was probably old and lazy in bed as well. So his treacherous young bride got to fooling around, and when she'd made enough friends in the banana business, she—and they—were ready to move. Nobody got excited when the old man died, probably a lot sooner than even an old man expected to. Little people don't ask questions. It would have been up to the old man's son and heir to demand an autopsy, and he was away at school. At least, everyone *thought* he was away at school. We'll never know whether her confederates killed him before the old man or not. Getting rid of him would have been even easier. Even if the younger Don Nogales had made friends in the States during his four years at Harvard, who's going to report a Honduran missing if they're told he just left for Honduras, right?"

Pru said, "How horrid! But if they murdered the real heir, who was that we just had dinner with, Dick?"

"Cuckoo chick numero uno. Doña Nogales herself was above suspicion, since everyone around here of importance had attended her wedding. When she in turn accepted her so-called stepson, who was in a position to argue if he'd sort of changed a lot in the past four years? Once the two ringleaders were set up with this plantation as a base, sneaking the other cuckoo chicks into the nest was easier. A few of the smarter local birds may have suspected something was up. The real Trader Breslin did for sure. But he played it too smart and too slow. He'd ordered a mess of arms he didn't want to pay customs duty on and alerted his own employees that something was up. But he held his cards so close to his gringo vest that not even his smuggling partner, Hardiman, knew what was really going on. Before Breslin could expose the charade, they replaced him with cuckoo numero dos, a gang member who looked sort of like Breslin and must have been able to sign his name even better."

"But, Dick, Mister Breslin hadn't been away to college. He must have been well known to many local people! How could they have hoped to palm a total stranger off as a local businessman?"

"Very, very ruthlessly. It was easy to get anyone in town out here to this plantation, a few at a time, simply by inviting them to dinner. It's not smart to refuse an invitation to the spider's lair when the spider owns the whole web. The servants were dismissed, the poison was served with the after-dinner brandy and cigars. Then other so-called business associates who'd been invited to the same party simply replaced the local big shots and, of course, their families. I know they must have mostly poisoned their victims because there were no bullet holes in the uniforms of those fake officers. Not when we sat down to table, anyway."

Pru shuddered against him as she said, "How ghastly! I feel better about those friends of Doña Nogales I sort of overreacted to, now. I can see how they'd have to replace anyone who could say anyone else was an imposter. But they must have been insane as well as murderous, Dick! How could they have hoped to get away with it, in the end?"

He held her a little closer to reassure her shivering flesh as he said, "They were doing pretty good when we got here. Naturally, an operation so big and bold had to occasion some conflicting rumors. The central government got wind of a lot of mysterious strangers hanging around a sleepy banana port with no visible means of support and sent Gaston and me to check it out. Gaston had passed through here, years ago, and knew some of the local rogues, as he calls them. With our reps as soldiers of fortune, it would have been easy to join a rebel group. But that wasn't what they were; and by the time we arrived, they'd made their final moves. So there just weren't any mysterious strangers to investigate. They'd all slipped into the identities of murdered and replaced locals.''

Pru frowned thoughtfully and asked, ''Then who were those so-called rebels the soldiers were rounding up and shooting just about the time we arrived?''

He said, ''The soldiers, of course. Once they'd replaced the officers and noncoms, the simple peon soldados never had a chance. The cuckoos simply ordered squads to isolated positions, threw down on them, then changed places with them. The killers stripped them of their uniforms and tarred and feathered them, lest someone attending a jolly public execution wonder why a familiar face was standing on the wrong side of the firing squad, and that was that. Once they switched the local government, the entire military garrison, the trading company, and the only plantation for miles, they had full control. Anyone else who even asked questions was in great shape to wind up executed as a rebel, killed by Indians, or just plain missing.''

Pru shook her blond head and insisted, ''It wouldn't have worked forever, Dick. Sooner or later the real army would have caught on. When my parents were on the road, I stayed with kin on an isolated outpost in the Dakotas. But no army unit is ever *that* isolated! There are always visiting inspection officers. The finance department checks the signatures on the pay books, and nobody would expect *every* private in a garrison to re-enlist when his hitch was up!''

He chuckled fondly and said, ''I was wondering how an actress learned to handle a gun so good. You're right about the military angle. But that was where the so-called Indian troubles came in. The local Indians, as you saw, were friendly. *Too* friendly for the imposters. They traded with the real Breslin. They knew the real young Don Nogales, and since they felt less cowed by aristocratic Creoles than mestizo workers who couldn't afford to voice even mild suspicions, the Indians had to go. At the same time, Indian trouble made a dandy rug to sweep more dust under. The gang used the shot-up trading posts as a handy place to dump leftover bodies.''

Pru cut in to ask, "Didn't the fake Breslin want the real one's Indian business, Dick?" and he said, "No. They were playing for higher stakes. The real Breslin had an import-export license issued by the Honduran government. Exporting bananas, through him, would avoid having to deal with old customers who might have bounced the young Don Nogales on a knee or two in the past. Blaming the Indians for wiping out the original trading business meant more bananas to export than ever, once the army naturally killed or drove the so-called hostiles off their tribal lands. The punitive patrol Gaston and me shot up weren't expecting to end their short army careers just that way. But after they wiped out that friendly, unsuspecting village of Chorti they were expecting to find, they would have simply changed back into civvies and drifted back to the plantation to go into the banana business. They meant to lose the rest of the local garrison the same way; then yell for help and get as many strangers to the area as possible here, poco tiempo. Then they'd . . . Hell, Pru, you're too smart to need diagrams, right?"

She nodded sagely and said, "Once the government thought it was dealing with a full-scale Indian war, they'd be too busy avenging their missing military martyrs to pay attention to the local banana trade. I can see how they might have gotten away with it, wild as the whole plan was, if you and Gaston hadn't been so smart, sneaky, and wild yourselves! Why have you got that hand on my knee, Dick?"

He said, "Sorry. Wasn't thinking. Sally told me about your, ah, unusual views, damn it."

Pru placed her own soft palm on the back of his hand before he could remove it and murmured, "Oh? And just what was this mysterious notion of mine that rates such a growly 'damn,' Dick?"

He said, "I can't think of a delicate way to put it. So, okay, Sally said you were a lesbian. True or false?"

Pru laughed incredulously and said, "But she told me *you* were a sissy, Dick! She said she'd caught you and that silly Ferris in the act, and . . . Good God! Why would anyone want to tell such tales if they just weren't true?"

He chuckled and said, "Divide and conquer, I guess. She must not have wanted us to . . . ah, get together like this."

She laughed like hell. But when he started moving his hand thoughtfully up her thigh as he hauled her in for a howdy kiss, Pru twisted her face away and said, "Wait! I said Sally was a big fibber. I didn't say I needed *proof* that you liked girls, you fresh thing!"

He let go of her fast. Not because of her maidenly act, but because he'd heard something moving around out front!

He rolled off the bed to drop behind the Maxim trained out the window. As he peered out into the moonlight, finger tense on the trigger, he spotted what he'd heard and laughed, saying, "It's just an armadillo digging for grubs in the front lawn."

Behind him, from the bed, the blonde asked thoughtfully, "Then all we have to worry about is how we'll ever while away the idle hours until the troops arrive?"

He snapped the safety catch as he shrugged and said, "Oh well, I missed lots of books in the library." Then he rose, turned, and when he saw she was calmly unbuttoning her bodice, added, "Forget what I just said. I sometimes shoot my mouth off rapid-fire too!"

Pru fluttered her long lashes in the moonlight and murmured, "So do I. But if we've only got twenty-four hours to kill, don't you think we'd better get started, Darling?"

Renegade by Ramsay Thorne

___#1		(C30-827, $2.25)
___#2	BLOOD RUNNER	(C30-780, $2.25)
___#3	FEAR MERCHANT	(C30-774, $2.25)
___#4	DEATH HUNTER	(C90-902, $1.95)
___#5	MUCUMBA KILLER	(C30-775, $2.25)
___#6	PANAMA GUNNER	(C30-829, $2.25)
___#8	OVER THE ANDES TO HELL	(C30-781, $2.25)
___#9	HELL RAIDER	(C30-777, $2.25)
___#10	THE GREAT GAME	(C30-830, $2.25)
___#11	CITADEL OF DEATH	(C30-778, $2.25)
___#12	THE BADLANDS BRIGADE	(C30-779, $2.25)
___#13	THE MAHOGANY PIRATES	(C30-123, $1.95)
___#14	HARVEST OF DEATH	(C30-124, $1.95)
___#16	MEXICAN MARAUDER	(C32-253, $2.50)
___#17	SLAUGHTER IN SINALOA	(C30-257, $2.25)
___#18	CAVERN OF DOOM	(C30-258, $2.25)
___#19	HELLFIRE IN HONDURAS	(C30-630, $2.25, U.S.A.)
		(C30-818, $2.95, CAN.)
___#20	SHOTS AT SUNRISE	(C30-631, $2.25, U.S.A.)
		(C30-878, $2.95, CAN.)
___#21	RIVER OF REVENGE	(C30-632, $2.50, U.S.A.)
		(C30-963, $3.25, CAN.)
___#22	PAYOFF IN PANAMA	(C30-984, $2.50, U.S.A.)
		(C30-985, $3.25, CAN.)
___#23	VOLCANO OF VIOLENCE	(C30-986, $2.50, U.S.A.)
		(C30-987, $3.25, CAN.)
___#24	GUATEMALA GUNMAN	(C30-988, $2.50, U.S.A.)
		(C30-989, $3.25, CAN.)
___#25	HIGH SEA SHOWDOWN	(C30-990, $2.50, U.S.A.)
		(C30-991, $3.25, CAN.)
___#26	BLOOD ON THE BORDER	(C30-992, $2.50, U.S.A.)
		(C30-993, $3.25, CAN.)
___#27	SAVAGE SAFARI	(C30-995, $2.50, U.S.A.)
		(C30-994, $3.25, CAN.)

WARNER BOOKS
P.O. Box 690
New York, N.Y. 10019

Please send me the books I have checked. I enclose a check or money order (not cash), plus 50¢ per order and 50¢ per copy to cover postage and handling.*
(Allow 4 weeks for delivery.)

_____ Please send me your free mail order catalog. (If ordering only the catalog, include a large self-addressed, stamped envelope.)

Name _____

Address _____

City _____

State _____ Zip _____

*N.Y. State and California residents add applicable sales tax.   11